FRUITS
OF THE
GODS

GEORGIY SERGEYEVICH GARBUZ

Published 2024

Printed in the United States of America

First Edition
ISBN (softcover): 978-1-963380-35-4
ISBN (e-book): 978-1-963380-36-1

For information, address:
Holzer Books LLC
8 The Green, Ste. A
Dover, Delaware 19901 USA

For information about special discounts available for bulk purchases, sales promotions, and educational needs, contact:
info@holzerbooksllc.com
+1 (888) 901-7776

holzerbooksLLC©

Contents

Chapter 1

The Ancient Empire of Ata

In the 14th century, at the heart of the Middle East, lay the vast and prosperous empire of Ata. It stretched across endless deserts, fertile plains, and rugged mountains, its borders safeguarded by towering fortresses and a mighty army that kept threats at bay. Strategically positioned along the lifeblood of commerce, the Silk Road, Ata thrived as a bridge between the East and the West. Merchants from Europe and Asia converged in its bustling marketplaces, trading silks, spices, and gold, enriching the empire as caravans wove through its cities like veins feeding a great body.

The empire's wealth and military strength were legendary, spoken of in distant lands with both admiration and envy. Yet, beneath this gilded surface, social inequality festered. The ruling elite, composed of noble families, wealthy merchants, and influential religious leaders, controlled every aspect of life. Their opulent estates and lavish palaces were symbols of the vast divide between the powerful few and the impoverished many. In the shadows of their grandeur, the common people struggled to survive, living under the burden of heavy taxes and labor, barely scraping by in an empire that seemed to grow richer by the day.

At the center of this empire stood its beating heart: the capital city of Ata. Encircled by imposing walls of stone, the city rose out of the desert like a jewel, its spires glittering in the heat of the midday sun. As one approached the city gates, the scent of exotic spices and roasting meats filled the air, mingling with the chatter of a thousand tongues. Camels and horses jostled through the narrow streets, their hooves kicking up clouds of dust as traders hawked their wares. Every alleyway and street corner seemed alive with activity.

To the north of the city, the grand palaces of the nobility stood in stark contrast to the rest of the capital. Here, amidst lush gardens and sparkling fountains, the wealthy elite lived in unimaginable luxury. Ornate palaces, adorned with intricate mosaics and marble pillars, gleamed in the sunlight. Flowering vines climbed the walls of private courtyards, where noblewomen in silken robes lounged, and noblemen plotted the course of their fortunes. These estates were secluded oases, far removed from the troubles of the common folk, their walls high and their gates heavily guarded.

In contrast, the southern quarter of the city, known to its inhabitants as the Sands of Poverty, told a far different story. Here, the streets were narrow and winding, the houses huddled together in ramshackle rows, made of crumbling mudbrick and weathered stone. The air was thick with the smoke of cooking fires and the cries of hungry children. This was the realm of the laborers, beggars, and orphans, where families of ten crammed into single-room dwellings and where survival was a daily battle. The slums overflowed with the disenfranchised, their faces etched with the hardships of life in an empire that promised prosperity but delivered it only to a select few.

Despite the growing unrest among the poor, Ata's prosperity was undeniable. Much of this wealth flowed directly from the hands of King Sergey I, whose reign had seen the empire's riches multiply tenfold. His policies of aggressive expansion and tight control over the empire's trade routes allowed Ata to dominate regional commerce. The empire's fertile lands yielded abundant harvests of dates, grains, and olives, while its gold mines filled the royal coffers. Silk from the East, pearls from the Arabian coast, and spices from India passed through Ata's gates, enriching those at the top while leaving the lower classes with only the crumbs.

King Sergey I was both revered and feared. To the common people, he was the protector of the realm, a ruler who had ensured peace and prosperity through strength. But to the nobles and merchants, he was a shrewd tactician, careful to balance the competing interests of power, wealth, and religion. Under his rule, Ata had never been more prosperous, but it was a prosperity that came with a price: the widening gap between the haves and the have-nots, a gap that was becoming increasingly difficult to ignore.

The capital city, though bustling and prosperous, was a place of stark contrasts—a microcosm of the empire itself. The gardens of the wealthy and the sprawling marketplaces teemed with color and life, while the slums told a different story of desperation and struggle. In every corner, from the grandest palace to the smallest hovel, whispers of discontent could be heard, a faint echo of the storm that would one day threaten to tear the empire apart.

But for now, Ata stood as a beacon of wealth and power in the Middle East. It was an empire at its zenith, its influence spreading far beyond its borders. Yet, beneath the surface, unseen to most, the seeds of change were beginning to take root.

Chapter 2

King Sergey I

At the heart of Ata's success stood King Sergey I, the architect of the empire's dominance. His rule was marked by a delicate balance of force and cunning, ensuring that both the internal and external threats to Ata remained at bay. Sergey was a king who knew the value of power, both in gold and in blood. His hands had shaped the empire, expanding its borders through military conquest and securing its wealth through careful alliances with the merchants and nobility.

King Sergey was not a ruler who relied solely on his advisors; he was a man of action. His youth had been spent on the battlefield, leading campaigns that crushed rival states and secured Ata's place as a dominant force in the region. Now in his later years, he governed from the grand halls of the Palace of the Crescent Moon, where towering columns of alabaster marble supported the weight of the kingdom's decisions. The palace, a symbol of his reign, stood at the highest point in the capital, a constant reminder to his subjects that their king watched over them, always in control.

But Sergey's reign, for all its splendor, was built on a foundation of strict control. Under his rule, Ata's government had grown into a machine of efficiency, but one that served the interests of the few. The king had little patience for dissent or rebellion, and his approach to governing was absolute. He wielded the army like a hammer, ready to strike at the first sign of unrest, and his network of spies kept him well-informed of the rumblings within his kingdom. To ensure loyalty, he placed the wealthiest nobles in positions of influence, granting them lands and privileges, while ensuring that no one became powerful enough to challenge his authority.

To the people of Ata, Sergey was both a father and a warden. Many saw him as the protector of the empire, the one who had led them through decades of peace and prosperity. His military victories were celebrated, and his decisions, though harsh at times, were understood to be for the greater good of the empire. Yet, as the empire's wealth grew, so did the cracks in the society he had built. The common folk, though loyal to their king, began to feel the weight of the inequality that defined their lives. Taxes on the lower classes were heavy, and opportunities for advancement were few.

Still, Sergey was beloved for his victories, and many feared his wrath as much as they respected his rule. His iron grip on the empire ensured that no dissent would grow large enough to pose a serious threat, but even he knew that unrest was brewing, especially in the southern slums. The poor quarters, where families huddled in crumbling homes, were becoming a breeding ground for anger and resentment. He had received reports from his advisors about small uprisings in neighboring regions and whispers of discontent from within the capital itself, but for now, those were manageable threats.

In private, Sergey knew the day would come when the empire's foundations would be tested. His mind often wandered to his sons, and the future they represented. Both princes, born of his blood, were as different as the sun and the moon. And it was this difference that caused him the greatest concern.

His eldest son, Igor, was the model of what Sergey expected in a future king. Trained in the art of war from a young age, Igor had proven himself time and again on the battlefield. He was his father's shadow in war councils, echoing the same stern views on military strength and governance. To Igor, the empire's survival depended on its army, its borders, and its ability to crush any threat—internal or external. He believed in his father's vision of control through force, and in many ways, he was a reflection of the old king himself.

Georgiy, on the other hand, troubled Sergey. The younger prince's interests had always been unconventional, straying far from the expectations of a royal heir. Where Igor saw the sword as the answer to all threats, Georgiy looked to the stars, the earth, and the mysteries of the world. His fascination with astronomy, medicine, and the sciences was tolerated by the king, but never embraced. In a world where conquest meant survival, Sergey struggled to see the value in his son's vision of a future where knowledge, not weapons, held power.

Still, Sergey loved both his sons, though he often felt the weight of their differences pressing down on him like a stone. He knew that when the time came to pass the crown, Igor would be ready, but he feared what might happen if Georgiy's ideas—wild as they seemed—gained traction among the people. His younger son's empathy for the poor and his desire to educate the masses were noble in theory, but Sergey knew that such ideals could easily unravel the tightly controlled fabric of the empire.

For now, however, the king's concerns remained unspoken. The empire was stable, the wealth continued to flow, and his grip on power remained strong. The day would come when decisions about the future would have to be made, but not yet. Sergey had ruled for decades, and he intended to maintain control for as long as his body and mind would allow.

As he sat upon his throne in the Palace of the Crescent Moon, watching over the glittering city below, King Sergey I allowed himself a brief moment of satisfaction. Ata was his creation, his legacy. But deep in his heart, he could not shake the feeling that the future—guided by the visions of his younger son—would bring a change he was not yet prepared to face.

For now, the empire stood tall, its walls unbreached, its people loyal. But the cracks were there, unseen by most, and Sergey knew that even the grandest walls could crumble under the right pressure.

Chapter 3

The Two Princes

In the towering halls of the Palace of the Crescent Moon, the destinies of King Sergey I's two sons were being shaped, each reflecting a different vision for the future of the empire. As much as the empire's subjects looked up to their king, they knew the future would belong to the princes. And those two princes—Igor and Georgiy—could not have been more different.

Prince Igor, the elder of the two, was every bit the image of a warrior prince. Raised from childhood to lead armies, he wore his armor like a second skin. His reputation as an indomitable general had spread far beyond the borders of Ata. Igor's presence was commanding, his towering frame and chiseled features cut a figure that inspired loyalty in his men and fear in his enemies. He was often seen in the training grounds, overseeing the drills of his soldiers, perfecting their battle formations, and preparing for any threat that might rise against the empire.

In Igor's eyes, the strength of Ata rested in its military, just as his father had taught him. To him, peace could only be maintained through the blade, and the empire's continued prosperity depended on the suppression of threats—both external and internal. The world was, after all, a dangerous place, and only the strongest survived. Igor's life had been one of discipline, focused on preparing to one day take the throne and lead the empire in the same way King Sergey had—through sheer force of will and military dominance.

Yet, while the nobles and generals revered Igor for his strength and loyalty to tradition, they whispered in private about his unyielding nature. Igor's resolve made him a perfect leader on the battlefield, but in matters of statecraft, his uncompromising views sometimes left little room for diplomacy. He believed that problems were solved with swift, decisive action, and this often put him at odds with the more tactful members of the court.

Despite his pragmatic nature, Igor was not without heart. His loyalty to his father and his people was genuine. He had no ambitions beyond the continuation of his father's legacy—a strong, secure empire, unchallenged by internal strife or foreign threat. He cared deeply for the soldiers who served under him, sharing in their hardships and rewards. To many, this made him not just a leader, but a protector of Ata's future. In Igor's vision, that future was built on the foundations of the past: tradition, power, and order.

Prince Georgiy, by contrast, walked a path that led far from the battlefield. From a young age, Georgiy had been fascinated by the natural world and the heavens above. While Igor spent his days training in the art of war, Georgiy was often found with his nose buried in ancient manuscripts or gazing at the stars through a brass telescope he had built with his own hands. His curiosity was boundless, spanning from astronomy and medicine to alchemy and architecture. In a time when superstition often clouded the understanding of the natural world, Georgiy's thirst for knowledge made him both admired and misunderstood.

Where Igor's presence was fierce and commanding, Georgiy's was calm and thoughtful. His slender frame and unassuming demeanor often led others to underestimate him, but those who spoke with him quickly realized the depth of his intelligence and his passion for progress. His eyes, always filled with quiet intensity, reflected a mind that constantly sought to unravel the mysteries of the universe.

Georgiy's vision for Ata was not one of military conquest or territorial expansion, but of enlightenment. He dreamed of an empire where education was available to all, regardless of wealth or status. He envisioned schools where the children of Ata—especially the orphans and street urchins who filled the southern slums—could learn astronomy, mathematics, medicine, and engineering. For Georgiy, the future lay not in the conquest of foreign lands, but in the exploration of the stars.

His most ambitious idea was the creation of the Space School Academies, institutions dedicated to educating the youth of the empire in the sciences, particularly astronomy. Georgiy believed that if humanity was to truly flourish, they would need to look beyond the earth. He was convinced that one day, the stars would hold the key to Ata's survival and prosperity, and that knowledge—not the sword—was the greatest weapon the empire could wield.

But Georgiy's ideas were seen as dangerous by the court. The nobles, merchants, and religious leaders, who held tightly to their power, feared the implications of his vision. Educating the masses, they argued, would disrupt the natural order of the empire. Knowledge, in their eyes, was a privilege of the elite, not a right of the common people. Many of the rich viewed Georgiy as a dreamer, naive and out of touch with the harsh realities of the world. They scoffed at his belief that the poor could ever contribute meaningfully to the empire's future.

Yet, while the nobility dismissed his ideas, Georgiy's reputation among the common people grew. His medical experiments, particularly his innovations in inhalation therapy for lung diseases, had saved countless lives, especially among the poor, who could not afford the traditional treatments offered by the city's healers. Word of his kindness and dedication to the sick spread quickly, and in the slums, Georgiy became known as "The People's Prince."

Unlike his brother, who was seen as distant and intimidating, Georgiy was loved for his empathy and his willingness to help those in need. Many whispered that, despite his eccentricities, Georgiy's vision could transform Ata into a beacon of learning and progress. But others feared that such radical change could destabilize the delicate balance of power within the empire.

And so, the two princes stood at opposite ends of a great divide. Igor, the warrior, saw the future as a continuation of the past—one where strength ruled and tradition was upheld. Georgiy, the visionary, dreamed of a new world, one where knowledge was the key to power and where every child could have a future beyond the constraints of their birth.

For now, they coexisted in uneasy harmony, their paths running parallel but never intersecting. But beneath the surface, tensions simmered. As their father grew older, the question of succession loomed large over the court. And with it, the question of which vision for Ata's future would prevail.

Chapter 4
The Empire's Social Order

Beyond the walls of the palace, the empire of Ata was a land defined by sharp divides—wealth and poverty, privilege and desperation, tradition and innovation. The upper echelons of society enjoyed lives of indulgence and security, while the lower classes toiled under the weight of a system that gave them little hope for advancement. It was a kingdom of contrasts, where fortunes were made by a select few and the vast majority struggled to survive.

At the top of Ata's rigid hierarchy were the nobles, a small group of wealthy families whose power was secured by bloodlines that stretched back centuries. They were the landowners, the military leaders, and the political elite, occupying the grand palaces and estates that dotted the empire's fertile lands. Their wealth came from vast holdings in agriculture—olive groves, grain fields, and vineyards—as well as lucrative trade deals. These families controlled the empire's resources and, by extension, its people. They maintained close ties to the crown, often marrying into the royal family to strengthen their influence. The nobles' opulent lifestyles were marked by banquets, hunting expeditions, and extravagant displays of wealth.

In the capital, the nobles formed a tight-knit circle of power around King Sergey I, providing counsel in matters of state. They were fiercely conservative, resisting any changes that threatened their control over land and wealth. While some of them respected Prince Igor for his military prowess and saw him as the rightful heir, they viewed Georgiy's progressive ideas with suspicion and disdain. To the nobility, the stability of Ata depended on maintaining the status quo—a rigid social order in which the rich ruled and the poor obeyed.

The merchants were another powerful class in the empire. Though not as aristocratic as the nobles, they wielded considerable influence through their wealth, which came from the thriving trade routes that passed through Ata. The capital city's bustling marketplaces were filled with goods from distant lands—silks from China, spices from India, gemstones from Persia. These merchants brokered deals that brought fortunes, not only to themselves but also to the empire, and they paid a hefty portion of their profits to the crown in taxes and bribes to keep their businesses flourishing. Though they were aligned with the ruling class, the merchants were pragmatic. Some saw potential in Georgiy's ideas for educating the masses, particularly as it related to advancing trade, technology, and innovation. But most viewed him as a well-meaning but naive dreamer, someone whose vision could disrupt the careful balance they relied on for their prosperity.

The religious leaders of Ata were perhaps the most enigmatic and conservative force in the kingdom. They held sway over the spiritual life of the people and played an essential role in maintaining order. Their temples and mosques dotted the city, their influence woven into the very fabric of Ata's governance. They preached about the divine right of the king to rule, reinforcing the idea that the social order was ordained by the gods and should not be questioned. Like the nobles, they saw little value in Georgiy's ideas for reform. Education and science, to them, posed a threat to the traditional ways, and they feared that opening the door to innovation might weaken their grip on the people's faith. Though they acknowledged Georgiy's intelligence, they preferred the certainty of Igor's steadfast loyalty to the old ways.

But it was in the lower classes that the empire's true heart could be found. The common folk, the farmers, laborers, artisans, and servants, made up the vast majority of Ata's population. They were the ones who worked the fields, built the palaces, and manned the trade caravans. Their lives were defined by hard work and hardship. In the capital, the poorest citizens crowded into the southern quarter, known as the Sands of Poverty, a sprawling district of crumbling buildings and narrow, winding streets. Here, families lived on the edge of starvation, struggling to make ends meet while the wealthy dined in opulence.

Among the most vulnerable were the orphans and street children, a constant presence in the slums. These children, often abandoned or left to fend for themselves, became thieves and beggars, doing whatever they could to survive. Many of them ended up in prison for petty crimes, punished for stealing food or begging for coins. It was these children, in particular, that Georgiy hoped to save through his vision of education. He believed that if given the chance, they could be the key to Ata's future prosperity, trained in the sciences, medicine, and navigation, and prepared to lead the empire into a new era of discovery. But for now, they remained trapped in the cycle of poverty and crime, invisible to the elite.

The working class also felt the growing divide between rich and poor. Farmers in the countryside struggled with rising taxes imposed by the crown to fund military campaigns and keep the nobility happy. Artisans and craftsmen in the city's bustling markets faced competition from foreign imports, while the guilds that once protected their rights were increasingly controlled by the wealthy merchants. The poor and the working class began to whisper about the growing inequality, but their voices were drowned out by the clinking of gold in the halls of power.

Georgiy, for all his idealism, understood the plight of these people. He spent much of his time in the poorer districts, tending to the sick and offering what help he could. He saw potential in the children who begged in the streets, the farmers who worked the land, and the craftsmen who built the city. In his heart, he believed that knowledge could change their lives, and by extension, the future of the empire. But the path to that future was fraught with obstacles, and he knew that his ideas, however noble, would not be easy to implement.

The nobles, the merchants, and the religious leaders had too much to lose. They feared that educating the masses would upset the balance of power and weaken their control over the empire. To them, a society where knowledge was freely shared and the lower classes could rise through education was a threat to their very existence. They had built their fortunes and power on the backs of the poor, and they were not about to let that system be dismantled by the vision of a prince who gazed at the stars.

Yet, even in the face of this opposition, Georgiy remained determined. He saw the empire as more than just a collection of wealth and power. To him, it was a place of limitless potential, a kingdom that could lead the world not only through military might but through enlightenment and progress. He believed that the greatness of Ata lay not just in its armies and riches, but in the minds of its people—if only they were given the chance to unlock their true potential.

The divide between the classes continued to grow, but so too did the hope that Georgiy's vision could bring about a new era. The question was no longer if change would come, but when, and who would be ready to embrace it when it did.

Chapter 5

The Seeds of Conflict

As the empire of Ata basked in its wealth and military might, cracks began to form beneath the surface of its golden age. These cracks, invisible to the nobility lounging in their grand estates, were growing wider by the day. The common people—those who labored in the fields, crafted goods in the city, and scoured the streets for a way to survive—could feel it. Beneath the glittering exterior of wealth and power, something was shifting. The empire had grown fat on trade and conquest, but it had also grown complacent. Unbeknownst to the elite, the seeds of unrest had already been sown, and they were taking root in the hearts of the people.

It began as a whisper in the crowded marketplaces, where merchants haggled over spices, silks, and gemstones. There, in the shadows of the towering minarets and opulent palaces, rumors spread. Stories of a different kind of future—one not defined by riches and power, but by knowledge and opportunity. These whispers spoke of Prince Georgiy, the younger son of King Sergey I, who had been seen in the slums offering aid to the sick and sharing his vision for an empire that uplifted its people through education and science. For the first time in generations, the poor and the disenfranchised had someone who seemed to care about their plight, someone who didn't just seek to extract from them but sought to empower them.

The people of the southern slums—the Sands of Poverty—began to see Georgiy as more than just a prince. He was a symbol of hope in a world that had long forgotten them. Children who once saw the streets as their only school now dreamed of attending the

Space School Academies, where they could learn not just to survive, but to thrive. The orphans and beggars of Ata, who had been invisible for so long, began to see themselves as more than the refuse of society. They started to believe that perhaps there was a place for them in Georgiy's vision, where knowledge could elevate them beyond their stations.

The whispers turned into murmurs, spreading through the city like wildfire. Soon, even the artisans and craftsmen, who had long felt the weight of foreign competition and the guilds' tightening control, began to talk of Georgiy's ideas. They saw the potential in his call for innovation and progress. What if we could build better tools? What if our children could be trained in the sciences? What if the future wasn't just about serving the wealthy, but about creating something new? The questions filled the air, and with them, the realization that change might be possible.

Yet, while the common people whispered of hope, the nobility and elite whispered of fear. To them, Georgiy's ideas were dangerous. His calls for educating the masses threatened the very fabric of Ata's social order. Knowledge, after all, was power, and in Ata, power was carefully controlled. The nobles had long ensured that education remained a privilege of the elite, passed down through bloodlines and carefully guarded within the walls of their estates. They feared that if the poor were given access to education, they might demand more—more rights, more opportunities, more power. Georgiy's vision, if realized, would disrupt the delicate balance they had worked so hard to maintain.

Among the elite, the merchants in particular felt uneasy. Their wealth depended on the continued flow of goods through Ata's trade routes and the strict control they maintained over commerce. Georgiy's ideas about technological innovation threatened to upend their comfortable lives. They feared that his push for progress would introduce competition they could not control, particularly if the lower classes gained the skills to challenge their monopolies. It wasn't just about education—it was about survival. And in their eyes, Georgiy's revolution would lead to the collapse of everything they had built.

The religious leaders were perhaps the most vocal in their opposition to Georgiy. For centuries, they had wielded immense influence over the people, ensuring that tradition and faith guided every aspect of life in Ata. They viewed Georgiy's obsession with science, medicine, and the stars as heresy. In a world where the heavens were seen as the domain of the divine, Georgiy's dream of space exploration was nothing short of blasphemous. To them, the prince was meddling with forces beyond his comprehension, threatening to disrupt the divine order with his radical ideas. They feared that his vision of a future guided by reason and knowledge would lead the people away from the teachings of the gods, weakening their grip on society.

As the elites of Ata gathered in their chambers, they began to plot against Georgiy's growing influence. In private, they warned King Sergey of the danger his younger son posed. "Your son may have noble intentions," they told him, "but his ideas will bring ruin to the empire. The people will rise up, and when they do, they will tear apart everything we have built." The king, ever pragmatic, listened to their concerns. He knew that Georgiy's vision for the future was at odds with the realities of ruling an empire. Yet, he could not dismiss his son entirely. Deep down, Sergey recognized that the world was changing, and he feared that if Ata did not change with it, the empire might fall.

King Sergey, for all his wisdom and strength, found himself caught between two worlds. On one side was Igor, his eldest son and the heir to the throne, a warrior prince who represented the empire's traditions of conquest and control. On the other was Georgiy, the visionary, whose ideas of progress and education represented a new and uncertain path. The king understood that these two paths were on a collision course, and he feared the day when the empire would be forced to choose between them.

The tension between the brothers was already palpable. Igor, ever the embodiment of tradition, saw Georgiy's growing popularity among the common people as a threat to the empire's stability. He believed that Georgiy's idealism would lead to chaos, that his brother's vision was too naive to survive the harsh realities of ruling. To Igor, the strength of the empire lay in its army and its ability to maintain order through force. He had little patience for his brother's dreams of space exploration and education. "The people need discipline, not dreams," he often muttered to those who sought his counsel.

For his part, Georgiy saw Igor as a relic of the past—strong, yes, but unwilling to see beyond the confines of the present. He believed that Igor's reliance on military strength would eventually lead to the empire's downfall. "An empire cannot survive on conquest alone," Georgiy would argue. "We must look to the future, to the stars, if we are to survive." The tension between the brothers, though not yet openly hostile, was growing. And those around them could feel it.

Even the common people, who had begun to rally behind Georgiy's ideas, sensed the impending conflict. In the slums of the capital, in the fields of the countryside, and in the workshops of the artisans, they spoke of the two princes—one who represented the old ways of power and control, and the other who promised a future of opportunity and progress. Many believed that a great reckoning was coming, that the empire would soon be forced to choose between its past and its future.

As the days passed, the tension in the empire grew thicker, like the air before a storm. King Sergey, ever watchful, knew that the time was approaching when he would have to make a decision. He had spent his life building Ata into a powerful and prosperous empire, and he would not see it torn apart by the ambitions of his sons. But as he looked out over the capital from the high walls of the Palace of the Crescent Moon, he could feel the storm coming. The question was not if it would break, but when.

And so, beneath the gilded surface of the empire's prosperity, the seeds of conflict were quietly taking root. The whispers of change, once faint and scattered, had grown louder. The poor and disenfranchised began to dream of a new future, while the rich and powerful prepared to defend the old ways. The stage was set for a confrontation that would shape the destiny of Ata.

What neither the nobles, the merchants, nor even the king could foresee was just how far-reaching the coming storm would be. For the forces that had been set in motion were not simply about two brothers or a single empire. The ideas that Georgiy had planted, the vision he had shared, were bigger than Ata itself. They were the seeds of a revolution—one that would reach into the heavens, and challenge the very nature of power, knowledge, and the human spirit.

In the quiet corners of the empire, in the minds of the people, a fire was starting to burn. It would not be long before that fire erupted into a blaze that would either consume the empire or transform it forever.

Chapter 6

The People's Prince

The empire of Ata, for all its prosperity and grandeur, was perched on the edge of a precipice, though few could see it. King Sergey I had built his kingdom on the twin pillars of military strength and economic wealth, confident that these alone would ensure its survival for generations. But beneath the surface, a quiet revolution was taking shape—one not fought with swords or soldiers, but with ideas.

Among the poor, in the slums of the Sands of Poverty, hope had taken root. The name of Prince Georgiy was whispered with reverence. The orphans, beggars, and laborers who had once accepted their place at the bottom of the social order now dared to imagine something more. Georgiy's vision of space academies and free education for the masses had inspired them in ways they had never thought possible. For the first time, they believed that they too could play a part in the future of the empire—if only they could seize the opportunity.

The fire of this hope, however, was as dangerous as it was powerful. The elites of Ata had spent centuries building walls—both literal and figurative—around their wealth and power. These walls had kept the poor in their place and ensured that the empire's riches flowed upward, to the nobility, the merchants, and the religious leaders. But now, the lower classes were beginning to see these walls for what they were: barriers to a better life.

The ruling class could sense the unrest, though they refused to acknowledge it openly. To do so would be to admit that their control was slipping, and this was something they could not afford to believe. But in their private conversations, behind closed doors in their palatial homes, the nobles and merchants spoke of "the People's Prince" with growing concern. "He is filling their heads with impossible dreams," one wealthy landowner would say to another, his voice filled with disdain. "Education for the poor? As if they could ever understand the complexities of governance, trade, or science."

The religious leaders, too, were growing more anxious. They had long maintained control over the hearts and minds of the people through the authority of the temple, preaching that the empire's social order was ordained by the gods. But Georgiy's ideas threatened to undermine this divine hierarchy. If the common people began to believe that they had the power to change their own circumstances, to rise above their station through learning and knowledge, what would that mean for the authority of the priesthood? The idea that the heavens could be studied and understood—let alone explored—was seen by many as a challenge to the very foundation of faith.

Tensions simmered within the palace as well. King Sergey I, for all his wisdom and experience, could feel the distance between his two sons growing wider with each passing day. He had tried to ignore it, hoping that time would smooth over their differences, but it was clear now that the divide between them ran too deep. Igor was the perfect heir in many ways—strong, disciplined, loyal to the traditions of the empire—but his rigid adherence to the old ways left no room for the kind of change Georgiy envisioned. Georgiy, for his part, was everything the king admired: intelligent, compassionate, and forward-thinking. But his ideas were dangerous, too idealistic for the brutal realities of ruling an empire.

The king often sat alone in the high towers of the Palace of the Crescent Moon, staring out over the city below. From his vantage point, the capital was a glittering marvel, its walls gleaming in the sunlight, its streets bustling with life and trade. But Sergey knew better than most that beauty could be deceiving. He had spent his life building Ata into the great empire it was today, but he feared that its foundations were weaker than they appeared. "How long can a kingdom survive when its people are divided?" he would ask himself. "How long before the cracks begin to show?"

Sergey had always been a king who ruled with strength, believing that an empire's power lay in its armies, its borders, and its wealth. But now, for the first time, he wondered if power alone was enough. His son Georgiy spoke of a future shaped by knowledge, not by force, and though Sergey dismissed many of Georgiy's ideas as impractical, he couldn't ignore the passion behind them. Georgiy believed in something greater—something that could take the empire beyond its earthly limits. "The stars," Georgiy would say. "The future lies in the stars."

But stars were far away, and Sergey had spent his life dealing with the hard realities of the world—battles fought on blood-soaked fields, alliances forged through marriage and trade, rebellions crushed before they could spread. He couldn't help but feel that Georgiy's head was too far in the clouds, too focused on the distant future to see the dangers that lay ahead. And yet, he knew that his son was not entirely wrong. The empire was changing, whether the nobles and merchants wanted to admit it or not.

The tension between Igor and Georgiy grew with each passing week. At first, it had been nothing more than sharp disagreements during the king's councils—Igor advocating for military expansion and stronger control over the provinces, while Georgiy pushed for reforms that would uplift the common people. But now, the divide was becoming personal. The two brothers, once close in their youth, could barely speak to each other without arguing. Igor saw Georgiy's ideas as a threat to the empire's stability, while Georgiy viewed Igor as an obstacle to progress.

The court, too, began to fracture. Advisors, nobles, and even generals found themselves quietly taking sides. Those loyal to Igor whispered about the need for strength in uncertain times, praising his military prowess and his ability to command respect. They saw him as the only logical successor to the throne—a leader who would protect the empire from external threats and internal dissent.

But others, particularly those sympathetic to the plight of the common people, began to gravitate toward Georgiy. They admired his compassion and his vision for a more enlightened empire. Even some of the younger nobles, disillusioned by the rigid traditions of their elders, began to see in Georgiy the possibility of a better future—one where power was shared, and knowledge was accessible to all.

In the shadows of the capital, the seeds of revolution were being planted. It began slowly, with small acts of defiance—disgruntled laborers refusing to pay their taxes, merchants quietly supporting Georgiy's call for reform, craftsmen discussing new ideas in secret guild meetings. The people were restless, and as their discontent grew, so did their loyalty to Georgiy. They saw him as the prince who would bring about the change they so desperately needed.

But Georgiy's growing influence was not without consequence. The nobles, merchants, and religious leaders began to press King Sergey to act. "Your son is sowing discord among the people," they would tell him. "He's filling their heads with dangerous ideas, making promises he cannot keep. If you don't stop him, he will tear this empire apart."

Sergey, caught between his love for his sons and his duty to the empire, knew he had to tread carefully. He could not afford to alienate Georgiy, not when the prince's ideas had already gained so much traction among the common people. But neither could he allow the foundations of his kingdom to be shaken by a revolution that promised more than it could deliver. The balance of power in Ata was delicate, and Sergey had spent his life maintaining it. Now, with his sons pulling in opposite directions, that balance was at risk of being shattered.

In the quiet of his chambers, Sergey often wondered what would happen when he was no longer there to hold the empire together. Igor was ready to take the throne, but could he govern with wisdom and restraint? And Georgiy—could he ever understand that idealism alone was not enough to rule? The king knew that the future of the empire lay in the hands of his sons, but he feared that their conflicting visions would lead Ata down a path of destruction.

And so, the seeds of conflict continued to grow, unnoticed by many, but clear as day to those who looked closely enough. The empire stood on the edge of something monumental, a change that would either propel it into a new era of enlightenment or plunge it into chaos.

For now, the city of Ata remained quiet. The streets bustled with the usual sounds of trade and commerce. The nobles continued to host lavish feasts, the merchants continued to make deals, and the priests continued to preach the eternal order of the gods. But beneath the surface, something was stirring. The whispers of revolution had grown louder, the tension between the brothers more palpable.

King Sergey could feel it, like the calm before a storm. And in the distance, he knew the storm was coming.

Chapter 7

Prince Igor

The desert sun hung heavy over the arid plains on the outskirts of Ata, casting long shadows across the battleground. Dust rose in swirling clouds beneath the hooves of warhorses as they thundered through the dunes, bearing down on the last pockets of resistance. Prince Igor rode at the head of his army, his sharp eyes scanning the horizon for any sign of retreat. His dark hair, streaked with sweat and dust, clung to his forehead, but his grip on the reins was as steady as ever. This was where he belonged—in the chaos of battle, leading his men to victory.

The campaign had been long and brutal, but Igor had driven the enemy back with ruthless efficiency. The rebellious province had once been a vital trading post along Ata's southern borders, but in recent years, its leaders had grown defiant, emboldened by the distant whispers of unrest within the empire. They had refused to pay the king's taxes and had taken up arms against the local governors, hoping to break free from Ata's rule. It had been a fool's gamble.

"They should have known better," Igor thought as he watched his cavalry sweep through the remaining fighters. "No one defies the empire and lives to tell the tale."

Igor raised his sword high, signaling his men to close in for the final charge. The sound of steel on steel echoed through the valley as his soldiers, hardened by years of battle, descended upon the enemy with merciless precision. The prince watched from atop his horse, his eyes cold and calculating, as the last remnants of the rebellion were cut down. There was no joy in his victory, only the satisfaction of a job well done.

To Igor, this was the essence of leadership—strength, discipline, and unwavering control. His father, King Sergey, had taught him that an empire was only as strong as its military, and Igor had taken that lesson to heart. Over the years, he had become Ata's greatest general, leading countless campaigns to expand the empire's borders and crush rebellions like this one. Under his command, the empire's enemies had been subdued, and Ata had grown rich and powerful.

But even as his soldiers celebrated their victory, Igor remained grim-faced. His mind was already turning to the next threat, the next rebellion that might rise if he didn't act quickly enough. "Strength is the only thing they understand," he thought. "If we show any weakness, the entire empire will unravel."

As the sun began to set, casting a red glow over the battlefield, Igor rode back to his camp. The war was over, but there was no rest for a man like him. Victory meant nothing if it wasn't followed by the swift re-establishment of order. He dismounted near his command tent, greeted by his lieutenants, who looked to him for direction.

"Send word to the capital," Igor said without hesitation. "Tell my father the rebellion has been crushed. The province will submit, or we will raze it to the ground." He paused, narrowing his eyes as he spoke to his closest advisors. "And make sure the leaders of this rebellion are publicly executed. The people need to be reminded of what happens to traitors."

His lieutenants nodded, their faces stern. They had long served under Igor's command and knew better than to question his orders. The prince ruled his army with the same iron fist he believed the empire needed. To him, mercy was weakness, and weakness was the beginning of the end for any ruler.

As his men dispersed, Igor turned toward the horizon, where the mountains of Ata lay in the distance. His thoughts shifted back to the capital, to the grand halls of the Palace of the Crescent Moon, where his father sat on the throne—and where his brother, Georgiy, was undoubtedly preaching his vision of progress and change. The very thought of it made Igor's jaw clench.

To Igor, Georgiy's ideas were nothing more than dangerous fantasies. His brother spoke of educating the masses, of uplifting the poor through knowledge and science. But what Georgiy failed to understand was that an empire could not be ruled by ideas alone. It needed strength—military might to protect its borders and crush dissent, order to keep the people in line. Georgiy's talk of reform and education was naive, a distraction from the real work of governing.

Igor had seen what happened when rulers let their guard down. He had spent years in the provinces, putting down revolts and enforcing his father's will. Every time he encountered a rebellious city or defiant noble, he was reminded that the empire's enemies were always waiting, always watching for an opportunity to strike. To Igor, Georgiy's dream of an enlightened, educated empire was a dangerous delusion. The people didn't need knowledge—they needed discipline, structure, and, above all, fear.

As night fell over the camp, Igor entered his tent and sat at his war table, maps of the empire spread before him. He traced his finger along the borders, noting the places where unrest had been reported in recent months. Small pockets of resistance, barely worth his attention for now—but if left unchecked, they could grow into something far more dangerous. He knew the court in Ata dismissed these threats as minor disturbances, but Igor had learned to see the signs. The empire was strong, but it was not invincible.

"We're one rebellion away from chaos," he thought grimly. "And if Father doesn't see that soon, it'll be too late."

He couldn't rely on Georgiy to understand. His brother's mind was too preoccupied with building schools and dreaming of space exploration to realize the dangers lurking within the empire. Igor respected Georgiy's intelligence, but he believed it was misplaced. Georgiy didn't understand the real world, the world of blood and battle, where every decision could mean the difference between life and death.

Igor's thoughts were interrupted by one of his commanders entering the tent. "My prince, the enemy's leaders have been captured. They await your judgment."

Igor rose, his expression hard. "Good. Let them serve as an example to anyone else who dares defy Ata."

As he stepped out into the night, the stars overhead glittered like distant fires, cold and indifferent to the struggles of men. Igor's gaze flicked upward for only a moment before returning to the earth beneath his feet. He didn't care for Georgiy's dreams of the stars. His duty was here, in the mud and blood of the empire. It always had been.

Chapter 8
Prince Georgiy

Far from the clamor of war and the blood-soaked fields where his brother reigned, Georgiy spent his days in the capital of Ata, surrounded by books, scrolls, and scientific instruments. The quiet hum of conversation in his study was a world away from the battle cries that Igor had grown accustomed to. Here, in the grand halls of knowledge that he had begun to gather around him, Georgiy felt more at home than anywhere else in the empire. The stars above and the minds around him promised a future that was still beyond the grasp of most, but one that he could almost see on the horizon.

Georgiy leaned over an intricate map of the night sky, drawn by his own hand. He traced the arcs of distant constellations, his brow furrowed in concentration. "One day," he murmured to himself, "we will understand these stars not just as gods' lights, but as places. One day, we will reach them."

His companion in the room, Amira, one of the brightest minds in Ata's small but growing community of scholars, looked up from her own research. "Prince Georgiy, your dreams are grander than most can comprehend," she said, her voice warm but tinged with concern. "The nobles mock your ideas. They say the stars have no bearing on the affairs of men."

Georgiy smiled, though it didn't reach his eyes. "The nobles," he replied, "are blinded by their own wealth and comfort. They forget that there is more to the world than what lies within their estates. Ata can be more than just an empire of swords and gold."

Amira nodded, but her eyes remained troubled. "You know that many in the court speak ill of your plans. They believe you to be...naive."

"Naive?" Georgiy leaned back in his chair, his fingers tapping lightly on the wooden desk. "Perhaps. But is it naive to believe that the future can be different from the past? Is it foolish to think that we can rise above conquest and war, that we can build an empire based on knowledge and innovation?"

He paused, staring out the window toward the sprawling city below. The capital of Ata, with its bustling streets and grand palaces, was the center of the empire's power. But to Georgiy, it was a city divided—between the nobles who controlled its wealth and the poor who lived in its shadows. He had seen it firsthand, walking the streets of the Sands of Poverty, the district where the empire's forgotten lived. Beggars, orphans, and laborers eked out their lives in the filth and dust, while just beyond the towering walls, the rich feasted in luxury.

It was those people—the ones ignored by his father and brother—that Georgiy thought of most.

"The world we live in now is ruled by strength," Georgiy continued, his voice growing more animated as his thoughts spilled out. "But strength alone will not carry Ata into the future. Knowledge, education, and progress will. If we invest in the minds of the people—if we teach them to think beyond the blade—we can build something far greater than this empire of gold and war."

Amira smiled faintly. "And the Space School Academies," she said softly. "You believe they are the key."

Georgiy's eyes lit up. "Yes. Imagine it, Amira—an entire generation of children trained in astronomy, engineering, medicine, and science. Not just the children of nobles, but all children, even those from the slums. Imagine what Ata could accomplish if the knowledge of the stars was not a mystery, but a reality. If the very people who now steal bread to survive could one day build machines that fly to the heavens. We could change everything."

He stood, pacing now as his excitement grew. "The stars are not distant gods," he said, gesturing toward the open window and the sky beyond. "They are destinations. They are the future. And if we educate our people, we can reach them. We can build ships that sail through the night sky, just as we built ships that sailed across the seas."

But even as Georgiy spoke, the reality of the situation pressed in. He knew that his ideas were met with resistance at every turn. The nobility, the merchants, the priests—they all saw his vision as madness, a distraction from the empire's real concerns. His brother, Igor, had made his contempt for Georgiy's ideas clear, dismissing them as childish fantasies.

The door to the study creaked open, and Vasil, a young apprentice scholar, stepped in, carrying a bundle of papers. His face was pale, and he hesitated before speaking.

"Your Highness," Vasil said, bowing quickly. "I bring troubling news from the court."

Georgiy stopped pacing, turning to face the boy. "What is it?"

"The Council of Nobles has been meeting without your presence," Vasil said nervous-ly. "They...they speak of you often. They say your plans for the space academies are a waste of the empire's resources. There are whispers that they will petition the king to shut down your projects."

Georgiy's face darkened, though he remained calm. He had expected resistance from the nobles, but he hadn't thought they would move so boldly. "Let them whisper," he said, his voice steady. "My father has not yet made his decision, and until he does, I will continue my work."

Vasil fidgeted, his eyes darting nervously toward Amira. "There is more, Your Highness. They are not just speaking against your projects. Some of them...they suggest that you are inciting rebellion among the people. They say that your visits to the slums and your talks of equality are stirring unrest."

Georgiy's expression tightened, but he remained composed. "I do not incite rebellion," he said quietly. "I offer hope. If the nobles see hope as a threat, that is their problem—not mine."

Amira stepped forward, her face filled with concern. "Georgiy, they are afraid of what you represent. They see your ideas as dangerous because they challenge the way things have always been. But if they convince the king that you are a threat..." She trailed off, the implication clear.

Georgiy turned back to the window, looking out over the city once more. The sun was setting, casting long shadows over the buildings below. The capital of Ata gleamed in the fading light, a city built on power and tradition. But Georgiy could see beyond the shadows, to the distant horizon where his dreams lay waiting. He knew the road ahead would not be easy. He would face resistance, perhaps even betrayal, from those who clung to the old ways. But he would not abandon his vision.

"My brother believes the future can be secured through force," Georgiy said softly, as if speaking to the city itself. "But I believe it can be secured through understanding, through the knowledge that we are all capable of more than what we are born into."

He turned to Amira and Vasil, his gaze steady. "Let them try to stop me. I will not be deterred. The stars will not wait for us to be ready. We must reach for them now, or risk being left behind."

And with those words, Georgiy's resolve hardened. He would continue his work, no matter the cost. The empire needed more than strength. It needed vision. And if no one else could see the future as he did, he would build it with his own hands.

Chapter 9

King Sergey's Dilemma

In the grand halls of the Palace of the Crescent Moon, King Sergey I sat upon his throne, but his heart was heavy. The king's crown, encrusted with gold and precious gems, felt like a burden on his brow as he watched his court around him. The nobles, gathered in small groups, whispered among themselves, their faces guarded but their intentions clear. They were waiting for him to make a choice—a choice that he had been avoiding for far too long.

King Sergey was a man of war, a ruler who had forged Ata into the powerful empire it had become. He had crushed rebellions, expanded the kingdom's borders, and secured its wealth through shrewd alliances and calculated force. Under his rule, Ata had flourished, but it had also become an empire of iron discipline. For decades, this was the only way he had known to lead.

But now, as his sons grew into men, Sergey saw the world changing, slipping through his fingers like sand in an hourglass. Ata stood at a crossroads, and the path the empire would take rested in the hands of his two sons—Igor, the warrior, and Georgiy, the dreamer. The king loved both his sons, but they were as different as night and day, and their visions for the future of the empire were pulling him in opposite directions.

Sergey leaned back on his throne, his eyes scanning the faces of the nobles assembled before him. He had spent decades earning their loyalty, keeping them in line with promises of land and wealth. Now, they looked to him to quell the rising unrest, to restore order as they had always known it. But the king's thoughts were far from settled. In recent weeks, his court had become a battlefield of ideas. Half the nobles demanded that Igor be named heir, that the empire's future be entrusted to a leader who could command respect through military strength and tradition. The other half, though quieter, spoke in whispers of Georgiy's ideas—of the prince's vision for an empire that could rise above conquest, built on education, knowledge, and innovation.

The sound of footsteps echoed through the throne room, interrupting Sergey's thoughts. His most trusted advisor, Chancellor Malik, approached the throne, bowing low. Malik had served King Sergey for many years and had guided the king through more than one political storm. He was a man who understood the intricacies of court politics as well as the hidden currents that flowed beneath them.

"Your Majesty," Malik said in his low, measured tone. "The Council of Nobles grows restless. They are concerned about the unrest in the southern provinces. Prince Igor has returned victorious from his campaign, but the situation remains volatile. Some of the nobles... they suggest that it is time to name an heir, to solidify the empire's future."

Sergey's jaw tightened. He knew the Council was growing impatient, but he had hoped for more time to consider his options. Naming an heir would not only settle the question of succession but would also signal which vision of the empire's future he intended to pursue—Igor's, rooted in the traditions of conquest and control, or Georgiy's, steeped in a desire for progress and reform.

The king looked out across the court, his eyes distant. "I know what the nobles want, Malik," he said, his voice heavy with weariness. "They want certainty, stability. But do they truly understand what is at stake? Do they see the world changing, or are they blind to it?"

Malik, ever cautious, spoke carefully. "They see what they wish to see, Your Majesty. They fear change, and they trust what they know—military strength, discipline, and order. Prince Igor embodies these values. He is, in their eyes, the natural choice to succeed you. But..."

Sergey turned his gaze to Malik, his brow furrowing. "But what, Malik? Speak freely."

Malik hesitated only a moment before continuing. "There are those in the court, and beyond, who are drawn to Prince Georgiy's vision. The scholars, the younger nobles, even some of the merchants—they see potential in his ideas. They believe that the empire's future lies not in war, but in knowledge. They speak of the Space School Academies as a bold step forward, a chance to elevate Ata to heights never before imagined. And then there are the common folk..."

Sergey's face darkened. "The common folk," he repeated, his voice thoughtful. "They speak of Georgiy as if he were their savior. They follow him, even though he does not ask for it."

"Indeed," Malik agreed. "The people love Georgiy because he offers them hope, something beyond the daily struggle for survival. But hope, Your Majesty, can be a dangerous thing. It can lead to discontent, even rebellion, if it is not managed carefully."

Sergey rubbed his temples, feeling the weight of his years pressing down on him. "And if I name Igor as my heir? What then? Do we crush these dreams of a better future? Do we turn the people against us by offering them nothing but more of the same?"

Malik's expression remained calm. "Igor is a strong leader, Your Majesty. He will ensure the empire's stability through strength, as you have done. But Georgiy's vision... if handled wisely, could bring prosperity in a different form. You are caught between two sons, each with a different path for the empire. The question is not just which son will lead, but which path you believe will carry Ata into the future."

Sergey sat in silence for a long moment, the weight of Malik's words settling over him like a heavy cloak. The king had spent his life building an empire, but he had never imagined that choosing between his sons would be this difficult. Igor was the natural successor—strong, disciplined, and unquestioning in his loyalty to the empire's traditions. He had already proven himself on the battlefield and had the support of the nobles. But Georgiy, with his idealism and his dreams of progress, represented something new, something untested.

"I have always believed in the strength of the sword," Sergey murmured, more to himself than to Malik. "It has brought us this far. But I cannot ignore that the world is changing. The people are restless, and the old ways may not be enough to keep them in line."

Malik inclined his head. "That is true, Your Majesty. But change, too, is a dangerous path. It can lead to greatness, or it can lead to ruin. The balance between tradition and progress is a delicate one. Prince Igor offers certainty, but Prince Georgiy offers possibility. The choice is yours."

Sergey leaned forward, his elbows resting on his knees, his hands clasped tightly together. He felt the weight of the entire empire pressing down on his shoulders. Choosing between his sons wasn't just about naming an heir—it was about deciding the future of Ata. Would the empire continue down the path it had followed for centuries, a path of strength and conquest, or would it take a leap into the unknown, into the world that Georgiy envisioned?

The king sighed deeply. "I cannot choose yet," he said quietly. "Not while the empire still stands at this crossroads. I need more time. Igor is strong, but I cannot dismiss Georgiy's vision, no matter how impractical it seems. The people believe in him. And if we are to survive the coming storm, we may need more than just the sword."

Malik bowed his head in understanding. "I will convey your wishes to the Council, Your Majesty. But I would advise caution. The nobles grow impatient, and the empire cannot wait forever for an answer."

Sergey nodded, though his heart was still heavy. He knew Malik was right—the time for indecision was running out. But for now, he would hold off, hoping that something, anything, would make the path ahead clearer. As Malik turned to leave, the king rose from his throne and walked toward the large windows that overlooked the city of Ata. The sun was setting, casting long shadows over the streets below. From his vantage point, the city looked peaceful, but Sergey knew better. The empire was a tinderbox, waiting for a spark.

He could feel the tension in the air, the unrest simmering just beneath the surface. The nobles wanted stability. The people wanted hope. His sons wanted two different futures. And he, the king, was caught in the middle.

"Which path will lead us forward?" Sergey whispered to the empty room, his gaze fixed on the distant horizon. "And which path will tear us apart?"

Chapter 10
The First Signs of Rebellion

King Sergey's indecision had not gone unnoticed by the people of Ata. While the court debated, and the king wrestled with his dilemma, unrest was quietly spreading across the empire. In the southern provinces, where the people had suffered from harsh taxation and neglect, small uprisings had begun to surface. These were not yet full-scale revolts, but they were enough to unsettle the nobility and worry the commanders stationed in the region.

In the provincial capital of Almosar, the signs of discontent had been growing for weeks. The streets, once bustling with traders and craftsmen, were now filled with whispers of rebellion. The local governor, an aging noble named Lord Khassan, had tried to maintain control, but his grip on the province was slipping. The taxes imposed by the crown had grown heavier over the years, and the common people had begun to question why they should continue to pay for a king who seemed so far removed from their daily struggles.

In a dusty tavern near the outskirts of the city, a group of farmers and laborers gathered in secret. They spoke in low tones, casting nervous glances toward the door, afraid of being overheard by Khassan's spies. The tavern's owner, a burly man named Rashid, leaned forward across the table, his eyes glinting with determination.

"The time has come," Rashid said, his voice barely above a whisper. "We cannot continue to live under the heel of the nobles while they grow rich off our labor. Prince Georgiy speaks of a better future—a future where we are not slaves to the crown, but citizens with rights. If we rise up, we can force the king to listen."

The others at the table exchanged uncertain looks. "But how can we rise against the king's army?" asked Yusef, a young blacksmith with soot-stained hands. "We have no weapons, no soldiers. We are farmers and craftsmen, not warriors like Prince Igor."

Rashid's jaw tightened. "We may not have weapons, but we have numbers. And we have Prince Georgiy's ideas. The people are hungry for change. If we strike now, we can seize control of the province before the crown even realizes what has happened."

The group fell into uneasy silence. For years, they had lived under the thumb of the nobility, their lives shaped by taxes and laws they had no say in. But the whispers of Georgiy's vision had reached even this remote province, and for the first time, they saw the possibility of something different. The question was whether they were willing to risk their lives for it.

"We'll need more than words to win this fight," said Hassan, an older man who had seen his share of violence in the past. "The crown will not sit idly by while we take up arms. And Prince Igor will crush us if given the chance."

Rashid nodded grimly. "Then we must make sure they don't get the chance. We need to move swiftly, take the governor by surprise. Once we have control of the city, we can send word to the capital. We'll demand that the king recognize our demands—or face a full-scale rebellion."

As the meeting broke up, the seeds of revolution were planted. It wasn't the first time the people of Ata had risen against the crown, but this time felt different. This time, they were inspired by something greater than just survival. They were inspired by the idea that a better world was possible, one where they could shape their own futures.

But as the farmers and laborers left the tavern, none of them could know the full weight of the forces they were about to set in motion. For while the rebellion in Almosar would start as a small, local uprising, it would not remain that way for long.

Chapter 11

Igor's Response

The first reports of unrest in Almosar reached the capital of Ata like a storm gathering on the horizon. Rumors had begun trickling in from the southern provinces—talk of angry mobs, overturned grain carts, and the governor's palace set ablaze. The whispers spoke of rebellion, of a province in open defiance of the crown. The moment the news reached Prince Igor, it stoked a fire within him.

Igor stood in his private chambers within the Palace of the Crescent Moon, surrounded by his commanders and closest advisors. His fingers drummed impatiently on the edge of a large, ornate table where maps of Ata and its neighboring provinces lay spread out. His face, usually a mask of discipline, was hardened into something darker—something closer to fury. "They dare defy the crown," he muttered, his voice low but filled with menace.

General Voronov, one of his most trusted lieutenants, cleared his throat as he stepped forward, handing Igor a report from the provincial garrison. "The rebels have taken control of Almosar, Your Highness," Voronov said. "They've overthrown Governor Khassan and seized the treasury. The leader of this uprising, a man named Rashid, has declared that Almosar will no longer be subject to the king's taxes."

Igor's hand clenched into a fist. "Khassan is a fool," he growled. "He should have crushed this insurrection the moment it began." His eyes narrowed as he stared down at the map of the southern provinces. Almosar, once a vital trading hub that linked Ata to the far reaches of its empire, was now a symbol of defiance. And to make matters worse, the rebels had invoked his brother Georgiy's name in their cause, claiming they were inspired by his ideals of equality and justice.

The very thought of it sent a wave of cold anger through Igor's veins.

"This rebellion must be crushed immediately," Igor said, his voice cutting through the room like a blade. "The longer we allow them to hold the city, the more emboldened the rest of the provinces will become. We cannot let this spread."

Voronov nodded gravely. "The garrison at Almosar is loyal, but they're outnumbered. We can have reinforcements ready to march within the day. With your permission, Your Highness, we'll send word to assemble the legions."

"Do it," Igor commanded, slamming his fist down on the table. "I want no mercy shown to these rebels. They've chosen their path, and they will pay for it with their blood."

The room buzzed with the movement of officers and aides, rushing to carry out the prince's orders. Maps were rolled up, and strategies were whispered between commanders, all while Igor stood motionless, his gaze fixed on the reports before him. His thoughts turned to his brother, Georgiy, and the growing influence of his idealistic rhetoric. This rebellion was more than just a local uprising—it was a symptom of the poison Georgiy had been spreading throughout the empire.

"This is your doing, Georgiy," Igor muttered under his breath. "Your words have given these peasants the idea that they can defy the throne."

Chapter 12

The Confrontation at Court

The court of Ata had never been a quiet place, but today it buzzed with an energy that was different from the usual politicking and whispered alliances. Tension hung thick in the air, filling the grand chambers of the Palace of the Crescent Moon. King Sergey sat upon his throne, his face drawn with the weight of the decision before him. Around him, the nobility gathered in tight clusters, whispering behind their jeweled sleeves, casting furtive glances at the two princes—Igor and Georgiy—who stood at opposite ends of the room.

It had come to this. The rebellion in Almosar had forced the king's hand. The Council of Nobles was divided, torn between the fierce loyalty they felt toward Igor and the troubling support Georgiy had garnered among the people and certain factions of the court. And now, for the first time in front of their father and the entire court, the two brothers would face each other openly.

The clash had been inevitable.

Igor was the first to speak. He strode forward with the confident air of a man who had spent his life commanding armies, his armor gleaming under the chamber's torchlight. His voice cut through the murmur of the gathered nobility like a sword slicing through air.

"Father, the rebellion in Almosar is an insult to your rule," Igor began, his voice booming. "They have defied the crown, and by doing so, they have defied you. There can be no negotiation with traitors. They must be crushed, their leaders executed, and the province brought back under firm control. Anything less will be seen as weakness, and it will only embolden other regions to rise against us."

He turned, his gaze falling on the assembled nobles, many of whom nodded in agreement. To them, Igor's words were not just the call of a prince; they were the commands of a future king. He represented the empire's strength, the continuity of its iron grip on power.

"The army is ready," Igor continued, his tone firm. "I will march at dawn and restore order in Almosar. This is the only way to preserve the stability of Ata. The rebels have invoked my brother's name, claiming they fight for the ideals he preaches. But those ideals are a poison—giving these commoners the illusion that they can dictate terms to the crown. They must learn that defiance has consequences."

The room fell silent as Igor's words hung in the air. For a moment, it seemed as if the matter was settled—until Georgiystepped forward. Unlike his brother, Georgiy wore no armor. He stood before the court in a simple robe, his hands clasped together, his face filled not with anger, but with a quiet resolve. His voice, though softer, carried just as much weight as Igor's.

"Brother," Georgiy began, his tone measured, "I do not condone the rebellion in Almosar, nor do I support violence in any form. But if you crush these people with your army, you will not end their suffering. You will only breed more resentment. They rose up not because they wish to defy the crown, but because they are starving, overtaxed, and forgotten. Their rebellion is a symptom of a deeper illness in the empire—an illness that cannot be cured by the sword."

Igor's eyes narrowed as he turned to face his brother. "You would have us negotiate with traitors?" he spat. "You would reward their disobedience with leniency? This is why you are not fit to rule, Georgiy. You do not understand power. Power is not given; it is taken. And it is held by those strong enough to wield it."

Georgiy did not flinch. "What I understand, Igor, is that an empire built on fear and violence will not stand the test of time. You may crush Almosar, but what happens when the next province rises up? And the one after that? Will you march from city to city, leaving a trail of destruction in your wake until there is nothing left of Ata but ashes?"

The court murmured as Georgiy's words spread through the room. Some of the younger nobles exchanged glances, clearly torn between the two visions before them. The tension between the brothers had reached its breaking point, and now, in this moment, it was spilling out into the open for all to see.

King Sergey, who had remained silent until now, finally spoke, his voice a deep rumble that commanded the room's attention. "Enough," he said, raising a hand to still the arguments. His gaze swept from Igor to Georgiy, and for a moment, the weight of his decision was palpable. "I have heard both of you."

He turned to Igor first. "You are right, Igor. A rebellion cannot be allowed to stand. The crown must remain unchallenged, and the stability of Ata is paramount. We cannot afford to appear weak."

Igor nodded, his face hard but victorious. He had won, or so he thought.

But then, King Sergey turned to Georgiy, his expression softening slightly. "However, Georgiy also speaks truth. The people in Almosar did not rise up out of greed or malice. They are desperate. Starvation, overtaxation, and neglect have driven them to this point. If we do not address the underlying causes of this unrest, we will face rebellions in every corner of the empire."

A murmur rippled through the court as Sergey's words surprised both sides. The king's statement was balanced, but it did little to resolve the growing tension.

"Father," Igor pressed, his voice growing colder. "Then what would you have me do? Shall we sit idly by while these rebels spread their poison to other provinces? We must act swiftly and decisively."

Georgiy stepped forward, his eyes pleading. "Father, I am not asking for inaction. But there is another way. Send a delegation to Almosar. Offer them amnesty if they lay down their arms, and promise to reduce the taxes that have bled them dry. Show them that the crown does not rule through fear, but through justice."

The court erupted into debate. Some nobles voiced their agreement with Igor's call for swift military action, while others—particularly the younger, more idealistic members—spoke in favor of Georgiy's plea for negotiation. King Sergey, caught between his sons, leaned back on his throne, his hands gripping the armrests.

"This rebellion must be dealt with," Sergey said finally, his voice steady but heavy with the weight of leadership. "Igor, you will march on Almosar, as you have planned. However, you will offer the rebels amnesty before the battle begins. Give them the chance to surrender, and reduce the taxes on the province as a sign of goodwill. If they refuse, then, and only then, may you crush the rebellion."

Igor's jaw clenched, but he bowed his head in obedience. "As you command, Father."

Georgiy's expression remained calm, but his heart sank. It was not the full negotiation he had hoped for, but it was better than outright slaughter. He nodded in quiet acceptance.

The confrontation ended, but the rift between the brothers remained as wide as ever. As the court began to disperse, Igor strode out of the chamber, his face set in grim determination. He had his orders, but he knew what he would do once he reached Almosar. Mercy was not his way.

Georgiy lingered for a moment, watching his brother leave. He had tried to change the course of events, but he could feel the storm building. Igor's path was one of blood and iron, and it would leave scars on the empire that might never heal.

As Georgiy turned to leave the chamber, his father's voice stopped him. "Georgiy," King Sergey called softly. "Walk with me."

Chapter 13

Aftermath of the Court Confrontation

The tension from the confrontation in the court lingered long after the nobles had dispersed. The halls of the Palace of the Crescent Moon felt colder, quieter. Igor had stormed out, his face a mask of barely contained fury, while Georgiy had remained behind, speaking briefly with his father before retreating to his study. The court was now split more than ever, divided between those who believed in Igor's strength and those who quietly supported Georgiy's vision of progress.

As Georgiy walked the long corridors back to his chambers, he felt the weight of the moment pressing down on him. He had known that his ideas were controversial, but to see them weaponized by the rebels in Almosar—his name invoked in the very rebellion his brother sought to crush—made him uneasy. He hadn't asked for this. He didn't want the empire torn apart in his name. All he wanted was to make Ata better, to give the people hope, knowledge, and the chance for a brighter future. Yet, everything seemed to be spiraling out of control.

As he entered his chambers, his close confidante, Amira, was already waiting. She had heard about the events in the court and could see the strain in Georgiy's face.

"How did it go?" she asked softly, though she already knew the answer.

Georgiy sighed, slumping into a chair by the window. "Not well," he admitted, rubbing his temples. "Father is sending Igor to deal with the rebellion, but he's ordered him to offer amnesty first. It's a compromise, but it doesn't change the fact that Igor's solution is always bloodshed."

Amira sat beside him, her expression thoughtful. "Igor won't offer them anything. You know that. He'll march into Almosar, and before the sun sets, the streets will be soaked with blood."

Georgiy looked out the window, his eyes distant as he stared at the bustling capital below. "I know. And what can I do to stop him? Father listens to him. The nobles support him. My words mean nothing when faced with Igor's sword."

Amira hesitated for a moment before speaking. "Your words mean more than you think, Georgiy. People are listening to you—the poor, the scholars, even some of the younger nobles. They believe in your vision. That's why the rebels invoked your name. They see you as their only hope for change."

Georgiy frowned, a deep crease forming between his brows. "But I don't want violence. That's not the way to bring about change. I never asked them to rebel. I wanted to offer them knowledge, not war."

"You didn't ask them to rebel, but they did because they believe in what you stand for," Amira said gently. "The people are desperate, Georgiy. They've been crushed by taxes, neglected by the nobles, and forgotten by the crown. Your ideas are the only light they've seen in years. But when people are cornered, they fight back. They just need guidance—guidance that only you can give."

Georgiy was silent for a long moment, grappling with the weight of her words. He had always known that his ideas were radical, but he had never intended for them to lead to open rebellion. Yet, if the people truly believed in him—if they were rising in his name—could he really stay on the sidelines?

"Igor will destroy everything I've worked for," Georgiy murmured. "If he marches into Almosar and slaughters the rebels, it will be the death of any hope for reform. The people will see me as weak, unable to protect them from the crown's wrath. They will give up on the idea of a better future."

Amira placed a hand on his arm. "Then you need to act. You need to reach out to the people directly, show them that you stand with them. If you don't, Igor will be the only voice they hear, and his voice speaks only of war."

Georgiy's eyes flicked toward her, a spark of determination igniting within him. "What do you suggest? I can't go against my father's orders. I can't march into Almosar and stop Igor."

Amira leaned forward, her eyes steady and resolute. "You don't need to stop Igor physically. You need to counter him with words, with ideas. You need to rally your supporters, the scholars, the commoners, the younger nobles who believe in your vision. Speak to them, publicly. Show the people that there is another path, one that doesn't end in bloodshed. If you don't, the rebellion in Almosar will be just the beginning. More cities will rise, more blood will be spilled, and Ata will tear itself apart."

Georgiy sat in silence, her words sinking in. She was right. He had spent too long hiding in his study, dreaming of a future that might never come. Now, the future was here, and it was demanding action. If he wanted to save Ata from itself, he would have to take a stand—not just against Igor's methods, but for the people who believed in him.

***

In stark contrast, Igor was already preparing for war. His chambers were a flurry of activity as soldiers, commanders, and aides rushed to finalize their plans for the march on Almosar. The scent of burning torches filled the air as maps of the southern province were laid out across the table, each marked with strategic points and plans for the coming battle.

Igor stood at the center of it all, his face hard as stone, listening to reports from his generals. He had no patience for negotiation or diplomacy. Almosar had defied the crown, and there was only one way to handle defiance: with fire and steel.

"The city is well-fortified," General Voronov said, pointing to the map. "But their defenses are old, and the rebels lack proper military training. We'll have no trouble breaking through their walls."

Igor nodded, his eyes scanning the map with the focus of a seasoned general. "We'll hit them at dawn," he said, his voice cold and sharp. "Strike hard and fast, give them no time to rally. Once we break through, we'll capture their leaders and make an example of them. The rest will either flee or surrender."

One of the younger officers, Captain Orlov, shifted nervously before speaking. "Your Highness, do you not intend to offer them amnesty, as the king commanded?"

Igor's gaze snapped to Orlov, his eyes narrowing. "The king commanded that I offer them amnesty," he said slowly, "and I will. But make no mistake—this rebellion will end in blood, one way or another. If they refuse my offer, I will raze Almosar to the ground."

Orlov swallowed hard, bowing his head in submission. "Yes, Your Highness."

Igor turned back to the map, his mind already focused on the battle ahead. He had no doubts about his course of action. Almosar would fall, and with it, any illusion that the people of Ata could defy the crown. But even as he prepared for war, a small, nagging thought lingered in the back of his mind: Georgiy.

"He's a fool," Igor muttered to himself. "A dreamer who doesn't understand the real world." Yet, despite his disdain for his brother's ideals, Igor couldn't shake the sense that Georgiy's words had already taken root in the minds of the people. It was a seed of doubt that gnawed at him, even as he steeled himself for the bloodshed to come.

***

Meanwhile, Georgiy's chamber was quiet, save for the sound of his pen scratching across parchment. He had taken Amira's advice and begun drafting a public address—a call for support, not for rebellion, but for unity. He needed to speak to the people directly, to show them that his vision wasn't one of violence but of hope.

He looked down at the words on the page, reading them aloud as he wrote.

"People of Ata, I come to you not as a prince, but as one of you. I see your struggles, I hear your voices, and I know that the time for change is upon us. But we must not let that change come through bloodshed. The future I envision is one of peace, of knowledge, and of justice. If we are to rise together, it must be through understanding, not war..."

As he wrote, Georgiy felt a renewed sense of purpose. The battle for Almosar was imminent, but it wasn't too late to change the course of the empire. If he could reach enough people, if he could show them that there was another way, perhaps the cycle of violence could be broken.

"Let Igor march," Georgiy thought. "But I will be the voice of the future."

Chapter 14

The March to Almosar

The following morning, as the first light of dawn broke over the capital of Ata, Prince Igor stood at the head of his assembled forces. His personal standard, a banner emblazoned with the royal crest, snapped in the brisk morning wind as rows upon rows of soldiers stretched out before him. It was a sight to behold—thousands of men, all clad in gleaming armor, their faces set in grim determination. These were the best of Ata's legions, veterans from the northern campaigns and seasoned warriors who had fought alongside Igor for years. Today, they would march south to put down the rebellion in Almosar.

Igor's horse shifted beneath him, its powerful frame restless for the coming journey, but Igor sat motionless in the saddle, surveying his troops. His dark eyes were hard, unyielding, reflecting the cold purpose that drove him. There was no doubt in his mind about what needed to be done. The rebels in Almosar had defied the crown, and such defiance could not go unpunished. Igor had been given his orders, and he would follow them—though he knew in his heart that any offer of amnesty would be little more than a formality.

At Igor's side, General Voronov rode up, his expression as stony as his prince's. "The men are ready, Your Highness," Voronov said, his voice steady despite the gravity of the situation. "We'll reach Almosar by nightfall if we keep a hard pace."

Igor nodded once, his gaze fixed on the road ahead. "We march now," he said simply. "The sooner this rebellion is over, the sooner the empire can return to order."

The command spread quickly through the ranks, and within moments, the legions began their march. The clatter of armor and weapons filled the air, the rhythmic stomp of thousands of boots pounding against the earth as the soldiers moved as one. Dust rose in great clouds behind them, carried by the wind as they left the capital behind and began their journey south.

***

As the miles passed beneath them, Igor's thoughts remained focused on the task ahead. His mind was a battlefield of strategies and contingencies, every detail of the coming assault meticulously planned. He had led countless campaigns in his life, and this would be no different. Almosar's walls would fall, and the rebels would be crushed beneath the weight of the empire's might.

But as much as Igor despised the rebels, it was his brother Georgiy who occupied his thoughts more than anything else. The very idea that Georgiy's name had been invoked by the rebels made Igor's blood boil. Georgiy's ideals—his vision of a future built on knowledge and compassion—were naive at best and dangerous at worst. It was Georgiy's words that had planted the seed of rebellion in the hearts of these peasants, giving them the idea that they could rise above their station.

"My brother is a fool," Igor muttered to himself as he rode, his fingers tightening on the reins of his horse. "He doesn't understand the world as it is. He dreams of a world that can never be."

But the people believed in Georgiy. That much was clear. In the taverns and markets of the southern provinces, Georgiy's name was spoken with reverence, his ideas spreading like wildfire among the common folk. They saw him as a savior, a prince who promised them a better life, a future where they weren't just cogs in the machine of the empire but active participants in its progress.

To Igor, it was madness. The empire didn't need ideas—it needed order. It needed strength. And the moment he reached Almosar, he would remind the people of Ata what true power looked like.

***

The city of Almosar was not the grandest of Ata's provinces, but it had always been a critical hub for trade, connecting the southern routes to the rest of the empire. Now, the streets that had once been filled with merchants and travelers were quiet, save for the occasional patrol of rebel soldiers, nervous and on edge.

In the center of the city, inside the hastily fortified walls of the Governor's Palace, Rashid—the leader of the rebellion—stood with his closest advisors, staring down at a crude map of the city. He was not a soldier by trade; he had been a merchant, a man whose life had been shaped by the deals he struck and the goods he moved across Ata's vast trade network. But the crushing taxes imposed by the crown had left him and his people with nothing. When the governor had refused to grant them any relief, Rashid had seen no choice but to rise against the empire.

But now, standing before his makeshift war council, Rashid could feel the weight of his decision pressing down on him like a mountain. His men were loyal, but they were not soldiers. Most of them were farmers, laborers, craftsmen—men who had never fought in a real battle. And soon, they would face Igor's army, a force so formidable it could wipe them out in a single day.

"We don't have much time," Rashid said, his voice low and grim. "Igor is coming, and he'll show us no mercy."

One of his advisors, a former soldier named Karim, stepped forward. "We've fortified the main gates and set up barricades throughout the city," Karim said. "But it won't be enough. The moment Igor's legions reach the walls, we'll be overwhelmed. Our only hope is to hold out as long as we can and force them into the narrow streets. Maybe then we can use the terrain to our advantage."

Rashid nodded, though he knew the plan was little more than a delaying tactic. They weren't prepared for this. They had risen in desperation, not out of a belief that they could actually win. But now, with the empire's wrath descending upon them, they had no choice but to fight.

The room fell silent for a moment before one of the younger rebels, a man named Yusef, spoke up. "What about Prince Georgiy?" he asked hesitantly. "The people say he supports our cause. Couldn't we send a message to him? Ask him to intervene on our behalf?"

Rashid sighed heavily. "Georgiy may sympathize with us, but he's still a prince of the empire. And right now, his brother is marching an army toward our city. Even if Georgiy wanted to help, what could he do?"

But the question lingered in the air, and Rashid could see the hope in the eyes of his men. They wanted to believe that Georgiy, the prince who had spoken of justice and equality, would come to their aid. They wanted to believe that there was a way out of this.

"Send the message," Rashid said finally, his voice tired. "But don't expect a miracle."

***

Back in the capital, Georgiy was still drafting his public address when the message from Almosar arrived. It came in the form of a hastily written letter, delivered by a young boy who had traveled day and night to reach the palace. The letter was smudged with dirt and sweat, its parchment creased from the long journey, but its message was clear.

"Prince Georgiy, we ask for your help. The people of Almosar rise in your name, but we face annihilation at the hands of your brother's army. You are our only hope. If you believe in the ideals you have preached, please, do not abandon us."

Georgiy read the letter in silence, his heart sinking with every word. He had feared this moment, feared that the rebellion would look to him for salvation. But how could he save them? He had no army, no power to counter Igor's might. He couldn't simply walk into Almosar and stop the battle with words alone.

But he couldn't ignore them either. The people were rising for him, and if he did nothing, they would be crushed—along with everything he had ever stood for.

He turned to Amira, who had been watching him carefully as he read. "They're calling for me," Georgiy said quietly, his voice heavy with the weight of the decision before him. "If I do nothing, they'll die. But if I go to Almosar, I risk being seen as a traitor to my father, to the crown."

Amira stepped forward, her expression resolute. "You've always said you want to change the empire, Georgiy. This is your moment. If you want to stand with the people, you need to do it now."

Georgiy looked down at the letter again, feeling the pull of destiny as if it were a physical force. This was his chance to prove that his ideals weren't just words. But it was also a chance to lose everything.

***

By the time Igor's army reached the outskirts of Almosar, the sun had already begun its descent, casting long shadows across the landscape. The city walls loomed in the distance, and from his vantage point, Igor could see the rebel forces scrambling to prepare for the coming battle.

He had given them their chance for amnesty. He had sent a messenger ahead with the king's offer—lay down your arms, and you will be spared. But even as the words left his mouth, Igor had known what the answer would be. These rebels, inspired by Georgiy's dangerous ideas, wouldn't surrender. They would fight, and they would die for their misguided cause.

As the army set up camp just beyond the range of the city's defenses, Igor stood on a hill overlooking Almosar, his jaw set in grim determination.

"Tomorrow, it ends," he said softly to himself, his eyes narrowing as he imagined the streets running red with rebel blood. "Tomorrow, the people of Ata will learn the price of defiance."

Chapter 15

The Battle for Almosar

The sky above Almosar was painted in shades of gray as dawn broke over the city. In the distance, the rhythmic thud of marching soldiers grew louder with every passing moment. The people of Almosar had long known that this day would come, but the reality of it was far more terrifying than they had imagined. From the vantage point of the crumbling walls, the rebel sentries could see the vast line of soldiers approaching—a sea of armor and banners marching under the imperial crest of Ata.

Inside the hastily fortified city, Rashid stood with his advisors in what remained of the governor's palace, staring at a map of the city spread out before them. His heart pounded in his chest, but outwardly he remained calm. He had chosen this path, and now there was no turning back. The people of Almosar had risen up in defiance of the empire, and they would fight to the last.

"They're almost here," said Karim, a former soldier who had been advising Rashid on military strategy. His voice was steady, but his face betrayed the grimness of the situation. "We don't have much time."

Rashid nodded, glancing up from the map. "Have the barricades been reinforced?" he asked.

"As best as we could," Karim replied. "The main gates are bolstered, but they won't hold for long. We've positioned archers on the rooftops, and the streets have been narrowed with makeshift walls. If we can draw them into the city center, we might be able to slow them down."

Rashid let out a slow breath, running his hand over the map. His plan had always been to drag the battle into the heart of the city, where the narrow streets and alleys would negate the advantage of the empire's larger, better-equipped forces. But he knew it was a gamble. Almosar's defenders were mostly farmers, blacksmiths, and craftsmen—men who had never wielded a sword before the rebellion.

"We fight with what we have," Rashid said softly. "We didn't ask for this, but we'll see it through."

***

The outer walls of Almosar were already crumbling when the first imperial forces reached the city. Dust and debris scattered as Prince Igor led his army forward, his gaze cold and focused. He sat atop his warhorse, towering over the soldiers who marched at his side, his eyes locked on the distant walls of the city. There was no room for hesitation in Igor's heart. Almosar had chosen its fate, and he would deliver it.

Igor raised a hand, signaling for the army to halt just out of range of the city's archers. Around him, the banners of Ata fluttered in the breeze, their imperial crest gleaming in the early morning light. The soldiers behind him stood at the ready, their armor clanking softly in the wind.

"They've fortified the gates," said General Voronov, riding up beside Igor. "But it won't hold for long. Once we break through, we'll push them back to the city center."

Igor nodded, his face impassive. "Begin the assault."

With that single command, the imperial army surged forward. The front lines carried massive battering rams, designed to smash through the city's gates, while the archers rained arrows down on the rebel defenders. The noise of the battle erupted in an instant—shouts, the clang of steel, and the groaning of wood as the rams slammed against the gates.

From the walls, the rebels fought back as best they could. Arrows flew from the rooftops, and stones were hurled down at the advancing soldiers. But it was clear that they were outmatched. The empire's forces were disciplined, their movements precise, while the rebels were scattered, disorganized.

"Hold the line!" Rashid shouted from behind the barricades, his voice hoarse from hours of shouting commands. He stood with his men at the city's main gate, watching as the imperial forces battered their way through. Sweat dripped down his face, and his heart raced, but he kept his sword raised high. They had to hold on—if they could just drag the battle into the narrow streets, they might stand a chance.

The first crack in the gates came with a splintering of wood, and Rashid's heart sank. The imperial rams had breached the outer defenses. The gates would not hold much longer.

"Prepare to fall back!" Rashid called, signaling to his men to retreat to the secondary barricades deeper inside the city. The plan had always been to give ground slowly, forcing the empire's soldiers into the maze-like streets of Almosar, but now, watching the imperial forces surge toward them, Rashid realized just how desperate their situation was.

***

By mid-morning, the imperial forces had broken through the outer gates and pushed into the city. The streets of Almosar, once bustling with traders and merchants, had become a battlefield. Imperial soldiers in shining armor clashed with ragtag bands of rebels, their swords flashing in the dim light that filtered through the city's smoke-filled skies.

Prince Igor rode through the chaos, his eyes scanning the battlefield for any sign of resistance. His face remained impassive as his soldiers cut down the rebels in the streets. He had seen battles like this before—he had led countless campaigns across the empire, crushing rebellions and expanding Ata's borders. This was no different.

But as he rode deeper into the city, something began to gnaw at him. The people of Almosar fought with a kind of desperation that he hadn't seen before. They didn't have the skill or the weapons to match his soldiers, but they fought with everything they had, as if the very future of their city depended on it.

"They're defending an illusion," Igor thought, his lip curling in disdain. "They think they can defy the empire, but they don't understand the power they're up against."

As he watched, a group of rebel fighters—a mix of young men and old—rushed forward from a side street, their crude weapons raised high. They crashed into a line of imperial soldiers, and for a brief moment, it seemed as though the rebels might push through. But then Igor's cavalry swept in, cutting them down with ruthless efficiency.

Igor's jaw tightened as he surveyed the aftermath. This rebellion, like all others, would end in blood. But even as he prepared to lead the final charge into the city center, a part of him wondered why these people had risen up in the first place. What had driven them to this madness?

***

At the center of the city, inside the crumbling walls of the governor's palace, Rashid stood with the last of his men. The battle outside had taken its toll, and they were exhausted, their faces streaked with dirt and blood. The imperial forces had pushed them back to their final stronghold, and now they stood at the gates of the palace, waiting for the inevitable.

"It's over," Karim said quietly, his voice filled with resignation. "We can't hold them off any longer."

Rashid nodded, his eyes hollow. He had known from the beginning that this rebellion was a gamble—a last-ditch effort to fight back against the crushing weight of the empire. But now, standing at the end of it, he couldn't help but feel the weight of failure pressing down on him.

"Send the women and children out through the hidden passage," Rashid said softly. "They don't need to die here."

Karim nodded, but neither man spoke of the fact that the passage wouldn't be enough to save them all. The imperial forces would find them eventually.

"I'm sorry," Rashid said quietly to his remaining men. "I didn't mean for it to end like this."

One of the younger rebels, Yusef, shook his head. "It's not your fault. We fought for something worth believing in. That's more than we ever had before."

Outside, the sounds of battle grew louder, the clash of swords and the shouts of soldiers echoing through the streets. Rashid took a deep breath, steeling himself for what was to come.

"This isn't the end," he said softly, more to himself than to his men. "The people of Ata will remember what we did here. They'll remember that we fought for them."

And then, with a final, determined look, he turned toward the gates, ready to face the empire's wrath.

***

By late afternoon, the battle for Almosar had reached its bloody conclusion. The imperial forces had overwhelmed the rebel defenses, and the city lay in ruins. Fires burned in the streets, and the bodies of fallen rebels and soldiers alike littered the ground. Prince Igor stood in the city center, his armor splattered with dust and blood, watching as his soldiers rounded up the surviving rebels.

Among them was Rashid, his hands bound in iron shackles, his face bruised and bloodied but defiant. Igor approached him, his expression unreadable as he looked down at the man who had dared to defy the crown.

"You're the one who led this rebellion," Igor said, his voice cold.

Rashid met Igor's gaze without flinching. "We rose because we had no choice," he said, his voice hoarse but steady. "Your taxes bled us dry. Your nobles took everything from us. We had to fight."

Igor's jaw tightened. "And now you will pay the price for your defiance."

With a single nod, Igor gave the order. Rashid and the other rebel leaders were dragged away, their fates already sealed. They would be executed publicly, as a warning to the rest of the empire.

As the sun set over the broken city, Igor stood alone in the ruins of Almosar, his heart heavy but resolute. He had done what was necessary—what was right for the empire. But even as the battle ended, a cold thought lingered in his mind: the rebellion had been crushed, but the ideas that had fueled it had not.

Chapter 16

Georgiy's Dilemma

As the final sounds of battle faded from Almosar and the city was left in ruins, the capital of Ata was far removed from the carnage. Yet, even from the lofty halls of the Palace of the Crescent Moon, Georgiy could feel the weight of the empire's unrest pressing down on him.

The letter from Rashid still lay on the table in front of him, its edges crumpled from the hours Georgiy had spent reading and rereading its desperate plea. The rebellion had invoked his name, but the rebels had been left to fight and die alone. They had believed in his ideals—of a better Ata, one that lifted the common people rather than crushed them beneath the weight of noble greed and imperial might—but what had Georgiy done for them? He had spoken out in court, tried to sway his father and brother with reason, but in the end, Prince Igor had been sent to deliver judgment in the only way Igor knew how: with the sword.

Amira watched Georgiy from across the room, her sharp eyes filled with concern. She had remained by his side throughout the conflict, a steadfast voice of reason and compassion. Now, as she saw the turmoil in his face, she stepped forward.

"You can't keep blaming yourself," she said softly. "You did what you could, Georgiy. You tried to convince the court to seek peace, but they chose war. The rebellion wasn't your doing."

Georgiy looked up from the letter, his expression strained. "Wasn't it? They fought in my name, Amira. They believed in the things I said—the hope I tried to give them. And now they're dead. All of them. Because I couldn't stop this madness."

Amira crossed the room and placed a hand on his shoulder. "You can't hold yourself responsible for what Igor did. He chose this path, not you."

Georgiy shook his head. "But I should have done more. I should have gone to them, spoken directly to the people, rallied support for a peaceful resolution before it came to this. But I stayed here, locked in this palace, while Igor marched to war."

The weight of the truth was crushing. Deep down, Georgiy had always known that his words could inspire change, but until now, he hadn't realized just how much people had already begun to look to him as a symbol of hope. That hope had turned to rebellion, and when the moment came, he hadn't been there to stand with them.

"What do I stand for if I can't protect the people who believe in me?" Georgiy asked quietly, more to himself than to Amira.

Amira's eyes softened. "You stand for something more than just one battle. The fight for Ata's future isn't over. Yes, Almosar has fallen, but the people's belief in change hasn't died with it. You've seen how many support your vision—scholars, artisans, even some nobles. They're waiting for you to lead. You can't give up now, Georgiy. Not when the stakes are this high."

Georgiy closed his eyes for a moment, trying to push away the guilt and frustration gnawing at him. Amira was right. The rebellion in Almosar was a terrible tragedy, but the empire's problems ran deeper than one city's defiance. The people of Ata were suffering, and the cracks in the empire's foundation were growing wider by the day. He couldn't afford to retreat into himself now, not when his vision for a better Ata was still within reach.

But there was another side to this—a darker side. Georgiy knew that his ideals of peaceful reform were at odds with the reality of an empire ruled by strength and fear. If he continued to push for change, it would inevitably bring him into direct conflict with his brother. And worse, with his father.

***

Georgiy had spent hours pacing in his chamber, debating his next move. He knew that time was running out—if he didn't act soon, the aftermath of the rebellion would harden the court against any possibility of reform. But he also knew that his next step had to be careful, deliberate. If he pushed too hard, he could risk alienating the very people he sought to help.

When he finally left his chamber, he went to see his father. King Sergey had summoned him earlier, no doubt to discuss the outcome of Almosar and Igor's victory. The thought of speaking with his father now filled Georgiy with dread. His father had always been pragmatic, a ruler who believed in stability above all else. To King Sergey, Igor's ruthless approach was a necessary evil, a way to maintain order in an increasingly volatile empire. But Georgiy couldn't accept that.

When Georgiy arrived at the king's chambers, the guards opened the doors for him, and he stepped inside. King Sergey sat by the window, his face worn and tired. The weight of ruling the empire had taken its toll on the aging king, and Georgiy could see it now more clearly than ever. The king gestured for him to sit.

"I know why you've come," the king said, his voice rough with age. "You're troubled by what happened in Almosar."

Georgiy sat down, his hands clasped tightly in his lap. "Father, what happened in Almosar was a massacre. Those people weren't just rebels—they were our subjects. They believed in a better future, and we let them die. You let Igor burn their city to the ground."

The king sighed, leaning forward with a tired expression. "It's not that simple, Georgiy. The empire is fragile. Rebellion cannot be tolerated. You think those people rose up

64

because they believed in your ideals, but they rose up because they were desperate. Desperation breeds chaos, and chaos will tear this empire apart if we don't maintain control."

Georgiy's jaw clenched. "So you believe control is worth the lives of innocent people?"

King Sergey's eyes hardened. "The empire is built on stability. Without it, we have nothing. The people need to know that defiance will not be tolerated. They need order."

Georgiy rose to his feet, anger bubbling beneath the surface. "And what about hope, Father? What about giving them something to live for, something to believe in? This empire is crumbling because we've forgotten the people who built it. If we keep crushing them under the weight of taxes and fear, there won't be an empire left to rule."

The king's gaze softened, but only slightly. "You're young, Georgiy. You believe in a world that doesn't exist—a world where ideals can change the course of history. But I've seen what happens when those ideals clash with reality. Igor understands that. That's why he's the only one who can lead this empire when I'm gone."

Georgiy's heart sank at his father's words. This wasn't the first time the king had spoken of Igor as his successor, but hearing it now, in the wake of Almosar, made it all the more painful. His father had already chosen his path, and it was a path paved with the broken bodies of those who dared to dream of something better.

"Igor leads with fear," Georgiy said quietly. "And one day, that fear will turn against us."

King Sergey didn't reply. He only looked out the window, his face lined with the weight of years and the burden of kingship.

***

Later that evening, Georgiy stood in the shadow of the Great Library of Ata, the heart of the city's intellectual and cultural life. Word had spread that Prince Georgiy was going to speak, and a crowd had gathered, filled with scholars, craftsmen, and common citizens who had come to hear the prince's words. Georgiy's heart pounded in his chest as he stepped up to the podium, his thoughts swirling with the gravity of the moment.

For so long, he had remained in the shadows, trying to change the empire through quiet persuasion. But after Almosar, he realized that wasn't enough. The people needed more than ideals whispered in court chambers—they needed someone to stand up for them, to give them a voice.

Georgiy took a deep breath, and then he began to speak.

"People of Ata," he called out, his voice carrying through the crowd. "We stand at a crossroads. Our empire, once the envy of the world, is faltering. We are ruled by fear, and those in power seek to control us with violence. But I ask you—what kind of future do we want for Ata? Is it one where we crush those who dare to dream? Or is it one where we lift each other up, where knowledge and justice reign?"

The crowd was silent, hanging on his every word.

"I know that many of you are suffering," Georgiy continued, his voice filled with emotion. "I have seen it in the streets, in the slums, in the provinces. You've been taxed, oppressed, and ignored. But we can change that. We can create a future where your children don't have to fight to survive, where they can learn and grow. This empire was built on the backs of its people, and it's time that we give them something to believe in again."

A murmur ran through the crowd as Georgiy's words resonated with them. He could see it in their faces—the spark of hope, the possibility of a better future.

"But we must do it together," Georgiy said, his voice rising. "We cannot allow violence to define our future. We must rise through knowledge, through compassion. We must rise together."

The applause that followed was thunderous. For the first time, Georgiy felt the true power of his words. He had always believed in his ideals, but now he saw the impact they could have on the people. And though the path ahead was fraught with danger, he knew one thing for certain: there was no turning back now.

Chapter 17

The Turning Point

The energy from Georgiy's speech had swept through the capital like a wave. The Great Library's steps were still crowded with those who had come to hear the prince speak, their murmurs echoing long after he had finished. The streets were alive with discussions of hope and change, of a future where knowledge, not fear, ruled the empire. As the evening turned to night, small groups of citizens gathered in taverns, marketplaces, and homes, sharing their thoughts on the prince's bold vision.

But not everyone welcomed Georgiy's words with open hearts.

Back in the palace, the noble class was growing increasingly uneasy. The prince's public address had stirred something dangerous—a sense of empowerment among the common people, a belief that they deserved more than their current lot. To many of the nobles, this was a direct threat to the order that had kept them in power for generations. And while some younger, more idealistic nobles had begun to rally behind Georgiy, the older, more entrenched families viewed his vision as nothing short of rebellion in the making.

***

The night after Georgiy's speech, the Council of Nobles gathered in one of the palace's grand halls. The room was dimly lit, filled with the murmur of voices speaking in hushed tones. The air was thick with tension. At the head of the council table sat Lord Kazimir, an influential noble with deep ties to the military. His sharp eyes surveyed the room as the council members took their seats.

Kazimir was no stranger to the currents of power in Ata. He had weathered countless political storms over the years, but this—this was different. Georgiy's ideas threatened to upend everything he had worked for, everything that had kept the empire stable.

"We must act," Kazimir said, his voice cutting through the low murmur of the council. "Prince Georgiy's speech today was nothing less than a call for revolution. He may speak of knowledge and compassion, but what he's truly doing is rallying the common folk against us. And if we allow this to continue, it will not be long before they rise against the crown."

There was a general murmur of agreement from the older nobles. They had watched Georgiy's growing influence with a mix of suspicion and fear, and today's speech had confirmed their worst fears.

"The people are beginning to look at him as a savior," said Lady Serafina, a matriarch of one of the oldest noble families in Ata. "If we do nothing, it's only a matter of time before they see us as the enemy. We cannot let this go on."

Not everyone in the room agreed, however. Lord Mikhail, a younger noble who had supported Georgiy's ideas for reform, stood to voice his dissent.

"With all due respect, Lord Kazimir," Mikhail began, "Prince Georgiy's speech was not a call for rebellion. He spoke of peace, of improving the lives of the people. Surely, as stewards of the empire, it is our duty to listen to these concerns. The people are suffering, and if we ignore them, we risk more uprisings like the one in Almosar."

Kazimir's eyes narrowed as he looked at the younger noble. "You are naive, Mikhail. Do you truly believe that this movement will remain peaceful? The people are desperate, and desperation leads to violence. Prince Georgiy may not intend it, but his words are stoking the flames of revolution."

"Perhaps revolution is what the empire needs," Mikhail said quietly, though his words carried weight in the room. "The world is changing, and if we do not change with it, Ata will crumble."

Kazimir slammed his fist on the table, rising to his feet. "Ata will not crumble! Not while I have breath in my body. This empire was built on strength, and it will remain strong. If Prince Georgiy continues to undermine the crown, then we must take action to stop him."

The room fell into a tense silence. The divide between the old and the new was stark, and everyone in the council knew it. There would be no easy resolution to this conflict.

***

While the nobles argued behind closed doors, the streets of Ata were alive with a different kind of energy. Georgiy's speech had sparked something deep within the people. For the first time in years, they felt a sense of possibility—a belief that their lives could change, that they could have a voice in shaping the future of the empire.

In the narrow alleyways and busy marketplaces, small gatherings began to form. Artisans, scholars, and even laborers who had once felt powerless now found themselves discussing ideas they had never dared speak of openly. "Georgiy is right," they would say, their voices filled with hope. "We don't have to live under the yoke of the nobles forever. There's a better way."

Amira, who had helped Georgiy prepare his speech, walked among these gatherings, listening to the people's conversations. She could feel the shift in the air, the way Georgiy's words had lit a fire in their hearts. But she also knew how dangerous this moment could be. The nobles were already looking for ways to undermine Georgiy, and if the people grew too bold, it could give Igor and his supporters the excuse they needed to crack down harder.

At one such gathering, she overheard a group of artisans discussing the idea of forming a union—a guild that would protect their rights and push back against the taxes that had bled them dry for years. They spoke of organizing a peaceful march to the palace, to show their support for Georgiy's vision of a reformed empire.

"A march could be dangerous," Amira said, stepping forward to join the conversation. The men looked at her with a mixture of respect and curiosity, knowing that she was one of Georgiy's closest confidantes.

"We don't plan to cause trouble," said Jalil, a stonemason with rough hands and a tired face. "But the people need to be heard. We need to show the nobles that we stand with Prince Georgiy—that we believe in his vision for a better Ata."

Amira's brow furrowed. She understood their desire to act, but a public demonstration so soon after Georgiy's speech could be seen as an escalation, and she knew that Igor's supporters were just waiting for a reason to crush this movement before it gained too much strength.

"If you march now, the nobles may see it as a threat," Amira cautioned. "Prince Igor and his allies will not hesitate to respond with force. Let Georgiy build support quietly for now. There will be a time to act, but that time isn't today."

Jalil exchanged glances with his companions, clearly torn. "We can't sit idle while the nobles plot against us. The people are ready to stand up. If we wait too long, we might lose our momentum."

Amira sighed, knowing how difficult it was to ask people to be patient when they had already waited so long for change. "Just give Georgiy more time," she urged. "Let him work within the system. The more support he gains, the harder it will be for the nobles to silence him."

Reluctantly, the men agreed, but Amira could see the tension in their eyes. The people wanted action, and if they didn't get it soon, she feared they would take matters into their own hands.

***

Later that night, Georgiy sat alone in his study, the applause from his speech still ringing in his ears. His thoughts were a whirlwind of hope and uncertainty. The speech had gone better than he could have imagined—the people had responded with passion, and for the first time, he felt as though he had truly reached them. But the consequences of his words were beginning to weigh on him.

As he stared out the window at the flickering lights of the capital, he heard the door open behind him. Igor stepped into the room, his presence like a shadow cast over the warm glow of the fireplace.

"You've stirred the hornet's nest, brother," Igor said coldly, his voice dripping with contempt. "Do you have any idea what you've done?"

Georgiy turned slowly to face his brother, his expression calm but resolute. "I've given the people something to believe in. They deserve a voice, Igor. They deserve more than fear and oppression."

Igor's eyes flashed with anger. "You've given them false hope. You've made them believe that the empire can be ruled by dreams and ideals. But this world doesn't work that way, Georgiy. Power is taken, not given. And the moment these people think they can take it, they'll plunge the empire into chaos."

Georgiy stood his ground, his voice steady. "It's chaos you fear, Igor. But chaos comes when people are left with nothing but suffering. If we don't give them hope, if we don't show them that change is possible, then yes, they will rise. But it won't be because of me. It will be because of you."

Igor stepped closer, his voice low and dangerous. "If you keep pushing, you're going to force my hand. And when that time comes, I won't hold back."

For a long moment, the two brothers stood face to face, the tension between them thick enough to cut. The conflict that had simmered for so long was now boiling over, and both of them knew that the time for words was running out.

"I'm not afraid of you, Igor," Georgiy said quietly. "But you should be afraid of the people you've been crushing underfoot. Because they're starting to wake up."

Without another word, Igor turned and left the room, his footsteps echoing through the silent halls of the palace. Georgiy watched him go, his heart heavy with the knowledge that his brother's path could only lead to destruction.

Chapter 18

The Fall of Almosar

The early morning mist still clung to the air in the outskirts of Almosar, but within the city, the chaos of battle had long since faded. What had once been a thriving trading hub was now a smoldering ruin. Buildings were reduced to ash, the streets littered with the bodies of rebels and civilians alike. Fires still burned in the distance, casting a red glow over the devastated city. The rebellion, which had dared to defy the empire of Ata, was now nothing more than a grim memory.

Prince Igor stood in the heart of Almosar's main square, surveying the aftermath of the battle with cold detachment. His army had done what it was trained to do—crush the rebellion, restore order, and make an example of those who thought they could stand against the crown. The imperial legions were now rounding up the surviving rebels, dragging them from the remnants of barricades and collapsed buildings. The few who still resisted were swiftly dealt with.

General Voronov approached Igor, his armor stained with dirt and blood. "The city is ours, Your Highness," Voronov said, his voice heavy. "The last pockets of resistance have been wiped out. The leaders of the rebellion are in custody, including Rashid."

Igor nodded, but there was no satisfaction in his eyes. The battle had been won, but it had come at a cost. The streets of Almosar were drenched in blood, and the city itself was a shell of what it once had been. Still, it was necessary. The people needed to understand that defiance would be met with swift and brutal punishment.

"Bring Rashid to me," Igor commanded, his tone as icy as ever. "It's time to make an example of him."

***

In what remained of the governor's palace, Rashid and his fellow rebel leaders had been shackled and lined up in the courtyard. Their faces were bloodied, their clothes torn and filthy from the battle. Despite their condition, there was still a flicker of defiance in Rashid's eyes as he was dragged before Igor.

The courtyard was eerily quiet as the prince approached the rebel leader. The soldiers surrounding the scene watched in silence, knowing what was about to happen.

Igor stopped in front of Rashid, his dark eyes boring into the man who had dared to lead an uprising against the crown. For a moment, neither of them spoke, the tension hanging in the air like a blade waiting to fall.

"You could have surrendered," Igor said coldly. "You could have saved your people from this." He gestured to the city around them, its streets filled with the aftermath of the slaughter.

Rashid, his hands bound in iron shackles, met Igor's gaze without fear. "We rose because we had no choice," he said, his voice hoarse but steady. "The empire bled us dry. The taxes, the oppression, the endless hunger... We had nothing left to give."

Igor's expression remained impassive. "You had the chance to surrender. I offered you amnesty, and you refused."

"Amnesty?" Rashid spat, a bitter laugh escaping him. "You offered us chains. You think we fought just to live as slaves under your boot? We wanted a life worth living. A life where we weren't crushed under the weight of your father's taxes or your brother's soldiers."

Igor's jaw clenched at the mention of Georgiy. The rebellion in Almosar had been fueled, in part, by his brother's ideals. Though Georgiy had never openly supported the uprising, the people had invoked his name, believing in the hope he had offered them. It was a hope that had led them to this moment of destruction.

"Georgiy filled your head with dreams," Igor said, his voice low and dangerous. "But dreams won't save you now."

Rashid straightened, standing tall despite the weight of his chains. "It wasn't Georgiy who made us rise. It was men like you. You rule with fear, with brutality. And one day, that fear will turn on you. You may have won today, but this empire can't survive on fear alone. The people will rise again, and when they do, you won't be able to stop them."

Igor stared at Rashid for a long moment, his face unreadable. Then, with a single, sharp nod, he gave the order.

"Execute him."

The soldiers stepped forward, dragging Rashid to the center of the courtyard. His fellow rebels watched in silence, their faces a mix of fear and resignation. As the executioner raised his blade, Rashid closed his eyes, accepting his fate. His final words echoed in the stillness of the courtyard.

"The people will remember."

And with that, the blade came down, and Rashid's rebellion came to its final, bloody end.

***

As Rashid's lifeless body fell to the ground, Igor turned away, his face a mask of cold indifference. The rebellion had been crushed, but the victory felt hollow. Almosar lay in ruins, and though the people had been silenced for now, Igor knew that the seeds of discontent had not been entirely uprooted.

As he walked through the city, past the burning buildings and the scattered bodies of the fallen, Igor's mind was already turning to the future. The rebellion had been inspired by Georgiy's vision, by his ideas of reform and equality. And though Georgiy had not openly supported the uprising, the people had rallied around his ideals. It was a dangerous influence—one that could not be allowed to spread.

Igor clenched his fists as he thought of his brother. Georgiy was naive, but his words had power. The people believed in him, and that belief could become a weapon far more dangerous than any sword.

"This cannot continue," Igor thought. "Georgiy's ideals are a threat to everything the empire stands for."

He had tried to ignore his brother's influence, hoping that it would fade with time, but after Almosar, it was clear that something had to be done. Georgiy's vision for the empire was too dangerous. It undermined the very foundation of Ata's power—its strength, its order. If left unchecked, it would lead to more rebellions, more chaos.

Igor knew what needed to be done.

As he mounted his horse and prepared to leave the ruined city behind, he turned to General Voronov. "Send word to the capital," Igor said, his voice firm. "I will return in two days. And when I do, we will discuss how to deal with this... problem."

Voronov nodded, understanding the unspoken message in Igor's words. The prince was not just talking about the rebels. He was talking about his brother.

***

While the fires of Almosar burned, the news of the city's fall had already reached the capital. The stories of the massacre, of the mass executions, spread like wildfire through the streets and alleys. The people spoke in hushed tones, afraid of being overheard by the soldiers who patrolled the city, but the words were on everyone's lips: Almosar had been destroyed. The rebellion had been crushed, but the brutality of the empire's response had shaken many to their core.

In taverns and market squares, the common folk whispered of what had happened in the south. Many were afraid, but some were angry. They spoke of Rashid and his men as martyrs, of the lives lost in the battle as a sacrifice for a cause greater than any one man. The nobles, too, were divided. Some praised Igor's swift and decisive action, but others were beginning to see the cracks forming in the empire's iron grip.

In the quiet corners of the city, among the scholars and artisans who had supported Georgiy's ideals, the fall of Almosar was seen as a turning point. They knew that the rebellion had been doomed from the start, but the brutality of its suppression had only strengthened their resolve. The people of Ata were growing restless, and they were looking to Georgiy for leadership.

***

Georgiy sat in his study, staring out the window at the city beyond. The news of Almosar had reached him just hours ago, and though he had expected it, the reality of what had happened hit him harder than he could have imagined. His ideals, the hope he had tried to give the people, had been twisted into something that led to bloodshed. And now, the city lay in ruins, its people dead or imprisoned.

"How did it come to this?" he whispered, his voice barely audible.

Amira sat across from him, her face lined with concern. "This isn't your fault, Georgiy. You didn't ask them to rise up. They made their choice."

Georgiy shook his head. "But they rose up because of what I said, because of the hope I tried to give them. And now they're dead. All of them."

Amira leaned forward, her voice gentle but firm. "They believed in you, Georgiy. They believed in the possibility of something better. And they still do. The people are looking to you now, more than ever."

Georgiy looked at her, his eyes filled with doubt. "And what am I supposed to do? Lead them into more bloodshed? I wanted to change the empire through peace, through knowledge. But now..."

Amira's eyes were steady. "You can still change the empire. But you need to understand that this will not be easy. Igor will not stop. The nobles will not stop. If you want to give the people a future, you're going to have to fight for it."

Georgiy sat back, his mind racing. He had always known that his path would be difficult, but the reality of it was beginning to sink in. Almosar had been a tragedy, but it was also a warning. The empire was more fragile than it seemed, and the people were beginning to see that. If Georgiy didn't step up, if he didn't lead them, someone else would. And that someone might not have the same vision for Ata's future.

"I can't let this happen again," Georgiy said quietly, more to himself than to Amira. "I can't let more people die for a cause they don't understand."

Amira nodded. "Then lead them. Show them the way forward. But know that the path ahead will not be without sacrifice."

Georgiy took a deep breath, feeling the weight of the moment settle on his shoulders. He had spent years dreaming of a better empire, but now it was time to turn those dreams into reality. And that meant confronting his brother, his father, and the entire system that had kept Ata in chains for so long.

He stood, his resolve hardening.

"It's time," he said quietly. "Time to act."

Chapter 19

Aftermath in the Capital

The news of Almosar's destruction reached the capital of Ata within days. Word spread faster than the imperial messengers, carried by traders and refugees who had fled the battle. The people spoke in hushed tones, fear creeping into their voices as they whispered about the massacre and the brutal methods employed by Prince Igor to suppress the rebellion. The entire city seemed to hold its breath, waiting for what would come next.

In the palace, the tension was palpable. The nobles had gathered in the grand hall, their expressions ranging from concern to outright panic. Some openly praised Igor's swift and decisive victory, seeing it as a necessary act to preserve the empire's stability. Others, particularly the younger nobles, were deeply troubled by the rumors of the slaughter. They knew that the rebellion in Almosar had not been born of greed or malice but of desperation, and the brutal response only fueled the flames of discontent.

Georgiy sat in his chambers, staring out at the city beyond the palace walls. The weight of the news had hit him like a blow to the chest. He had expected the worst when Igor was sent to suppress the rebellion, but the reality was far worse than he had imagined. The streets of Almosar, once filled with life, were now drenched in blood. The people who had believed in him, who had taken his ideals to heart, were dead or captured.

"How many more must die before this is over?" Georgiy whispered to himself, his voice heavy with sorrow.

Amira entered the room, her face drawn and serious. She had heard the same reports, and though she had tried to console Georgiy, there was little she could say to ease his grief.

"The nobles are talking," she said quietly, moving to stand beside him at the window. "Many are worried about the unrest. Almosar was just the beginning—there are whispers of more uprisings in the provinces. The people are angry, and Igor's methods are only making it worse."

Georgiy nodded but remained silent. His mind was racing, trying to make sense of the chaos that was unraveling around him. The empire was cracking at its seams, and he could see the fault lines widening with every passing day. He had tried to bring about change peacefully, but the massacre at Almosar had shown him that his brother and the conservative nobles would never allow his vision to flourish. Not without a fight.

"I can't let this happen again," Georgiy said finally, his voice firm but pained. "The people are suffering, and if we don't do something soon, the entire empire will collapse."

Amira placed a hand on his arm, her gaze steady. "What do you plan to do?"

Georgiy turned away from the window, his eyes filled with determination. "I've tried to work within the system, to convince my father and the court that reform is necessary. But they've refused to listen. If I want to protect the people, if I want to create a better future for Ata, I can't rely on words alone anymore."

Amira frowned, sensing the shift in his tone. "You're talking about rebellion."

Georgiy looked at her, the weight of the decision heavy on his shoulders. "I don't want to lead a rebellion. I never wanted violence. But Igor has left me no choice. If the people rise again, I have to be there to guide them, to prevent more bloodshed. If I don't act, Igor will destroy everything."

Amira studied his face, searching for any sign of hesitation. There was none. Georgiy had always been the idealist, the one who believed that change could come through education, through enlightenment. But now, she saw a different side of him—a man who had been pushed too far, who had been forced to face the harsh reality that ideals alone could not save the empire.

"Then we'll need to move carefully," Amira said. "The nobles are divided, and the people are already looking to you. But we can't act too soon. If we rise before we're ready, Igor will crush us, just like he did in Almosar."

Georgiy nodded. "I know. But the clock is ticking, Amira. We don't have much time before this empire tears itself apart."

***

Meanwhile, in the grand hall of the palace, the court was in turmoil. The conservative nobles, led by Lord Kazimir, had gathered to discuss the fallout from Almosar. Though they praised Igor for his decisive action, they could not ignore the growing unrest among the people. The brutal suppression of the rebellion had sent shockwaves through the empire, and even the most loyal supporters of the crown knew that something had to be done to prevent further uprisings.

"Prince Igor has restored order to Almosar," Kazimir said, his voice booming across the hall. "But the people are still restless. We cannot allow these uprisings to spread. If we show weakness now, the entire empire will rise against us."

Lady Serafina, one of the older nobles who had long been a supporter of King Sergey's rule, spoke up. "And what do you propose, Kazimir? More bloodshed? The people are not our enemies. They are suffering under the weight of taxes and oppression. If we continue to rule with fear, we will only drive them further into rebellion."

Kazimir scowled, his sharp features twisting with disdain. "This is not about taxes. This is about control. The people have been led astray by dangerous ideas—ideas planted by Prince Georgiy and his supporters. If we allow his vision of the empire to take root, we will lose everything. This empire was built on strength, and strength is the only thing that will keep it standing."

The hall fell into tense silence as the nobles exchanged uneasy glances. The divide between those who supported Georgiy's ideals of reform and those who clung to the old ways had grown wider than ever.

***

As the court argued, the doors to the hall swung open, and Prince Igor entered. His presence commanded immediate attention. His armor was still stained with the dust of battle, his face set in a hard, unreadable expression. The nobles quieted as he strode to the center of the room, his dark eyes sweeping over the assembled lords and ladies.

Igor stood before them, his voice cold and steady. "Almosar has been dealt with. The rebellion is over."

Lord Kazimir nodded approvingly. "You've done well, Your Highness. But the people are still talking. There are rumors of more uprisings in the provinces. We must act before they spread."

Igor's gaze shifted to Kazimir, and for a moment, the tension in the room grew even thicker. "There will be no more uprisings," Igor said sharply. "I will ensure that the people understand the price of defiance."

The nobles murmured among themselves, some clearly uncomfortable with Igor's brutal approach. But none dared to speak against him. Igor had proven himself as a capable and ruthless leader, and they knew that crossing him would be dangerous.

***

That night, after the council meeting, Igor sought out Georgiy. He found his brother in the palace gardens, standing alone beneath the stars. The tension between them had been simmering for years, but Almosar had pushed them to the brink. Now, it seemed there was no turning back.

Igor approached silently, his presence dark and imposing. "You've been awfully quiet since Almosar," he said, his voice low and accusatory. "I expected more outrage from you, considering how many of your supporters were involved."

Georgiy turned to face him, his expression calm but determined. "I don't condone violence, Igor. You know that. But what happened in Almosar wasn't justice—it was a massacre."

Igor's eyes flashed with anger. "It was necessary. You've filled the people's heads with dreams, Georgiy. Dreams of a world that doesn't exist. And now they're willing to die for it. Is that what you wanted?"

Georgiy's jaw tightened. "What I want is for the people to have a future worth living for. A future where they aren't crushed under the weight of taxes and fear. But you've turned this empire into a prison, and you're surprised when they try to break free?"

Igor stepped closer, his voice a dangerous whisper. "I've kept this empire standing. I've maintained order, while you've been spouting your ideals to anyone who will listen. But ideals don't keep an empire together. Strength does. And if you continue to undermine that strength, I will stop you. Do you understand?"

For a long moment, the two brothers stood face to face, the gulf between them deeper than ever. Georgiy could see the resolve in Igor's eyes, the willingness to do whatever it took to preserve his vision of the empire. But Georgiy wasn't afraid.

"If you keep ruling with fear," Georgiy said quietly, "this empire will fall. And when it does, no amount of strength will save you."

Igor's expression darkened, and without another word, he turned and left the garden, his footsteps echoing in the quiet night.

Chapter 20

The Court Divides

The air in the grand hall of the Palace of the Crescent Moon was thick with tension. The nobles had gathered once more, their conversations hushed and nervous as they waited for King Sergey to appear. But it wasn't the king they were truly focused on—it was the growing divide between his sons, and the uncertainty over the future of Ata. The fall of Almosar had shaken the empire to its core, and everyone in the court knew that the time for choosing sides was fast approaching.

Lord Kazimir sat at the head of one of the long tables, his fingers tapping impatiently on the polished wood. He had long been a staunch supporter of the old order, loyal to King Sergey and the conservative vision of the empire that Prince Igor embodied. But even he couldn't ignore the growing unrest. The rumors of new uprisings in the southern provinces had reached the court, and Kazimir knew that it was only a matter of time before the rebellion spread.

Across the hall, Lord Mikhail, one of the younger nobles who had aligned himself with Georgiy's ideals, watched Kazimir carefully. He had seen the way the court was shifting, the quiet support growing for Georgiy's vision of reform. Many of the younger nobles, who had grown tired of the empire's harsh policies, were beginning to see Georgiy as the only hope for a future where the people were treated with dignity and respect. But they also knew the danger that came with supporting him.

"It's time we choose," Mikhail said quietly to the group of nobles gathered around him. "If we continue to sit on the sidelines, Igor will destroy everything. The people are already on edge. We need to support Georgiy now, before it's too late."

Lady Serafina, an older noble who had remained neutral in the conflict, raised an eyebrow at Mikhail's bold statement. "And how do you propose we do that, Lord Mikhail? Prince Igor commands the imperial army. If we openly support Georgiy, we risk war. The king may not survive that."

Mikhail frowned, his eyes dark with frustration. "The king is already losing his grip on the empire. He's too old, too ill to stop what's coming. If we don't act soon, Igor will take control, and any hope for a peaceful future will die with him."

There was a murmur of agreement from the younger nobles, but the older generation remained cautious. They had seen what rebellion could do—what it had done to Almosar. Supporting Georgiy was a risk, but so was remaining neutral.

***

While the nobles debated, King Sergey sat in his private chambers, far removed from the growing storm that swirled around him. His health had deteriorated rapidly over the past few months, and the weight of ruling the empire was becoming too much for him to bear. His once sharp mind was clouded with fatigue, and though he still held the title of king, it was clear that the real power in Ata was slipping away.

"Your Majesty," one of his attendants said softly, approaching the king's bedside. "The nobles are gathered in the grand hall. They are awaiting your guidance."

King Sergey waved the attendant away, his voice weak and raspy. "Let them wait." He closed his eyes, sinking deeper into the pillows. "I have nothing left to give them."

In truth, Sergey had known for some time that his sons were destined to clash. Georgiy's ideals had always been at odds with Igor's iron-fisted approach, but Sergey had hoped to keep the peace between them for the sake of the empire. Now, with Almosar in ruins and the empire on the brink of rebellion, he feared that his time was running out—and with it, any chance of preventing the civil war that loomed on the horizon.

***

As the court grew more divided, Georgiy was gathering his allies in secret. In a quiet villa on the outskirts of the capital, far from the prying eyes of the court, he met with a group of scholars, young nobles, and former rebels—those who believed in his vision for a new Ata. Amira stood at his side, her presence a constant source of strength and guidance.

The room was filled with nervous energy as the group discussed their next move. Georgiy had always hoped to avoid violence, but after the fall of Almosar, he knew that peaceful reform was no longer an option. The empire was changing, and if they didn't act soon, Igor would crush any chance of a future built on knowledge and progress.

"We need to build alliances," Georgiy said, addressing the group. "The nobles are divided, but many still sit on the fence. If we can convince them that there is a path forward without bloodshed, we might be able to avoid a full-scale civil war."

Lord Mikhail, who had joined Georgiy's cause after the massacre at Almosar, nodded in agreement. "We have support among the younger nobles, but we need more than that. We need the people. The scholars, the artisans, the merchants—they're all looking to you for leadership. If we can rally them, we can force the court to listen."

Amira, ever the voice of reason, interjected. "But we must be careful. If we move too quickly, Igor will strike. We can't afford another Almosar. We need to be sure that when we act, we are ready."

Georgiy nodded, his face somber. "I know. But time is running out. Igor won't sit idly by while we build support. He will act soon, and when he does, we need to be prepared."

***

As Georgiy gathered his allies, Igor was preparing for something far more direct. In the depths of the imperial barracks, he stood before his generals, outlining his plan to crush the growing unrest in the capital and the provinces. He knew that Georgiy was building support, and though he hadn't yet openly declared his intentions, Igor wasn't willing to wait for his brother to make the first move.

"The people are restless," Igor said, his voice sharp and commanding. "We've seen what happens when they're led by foolish ideals. Almosar was just the beginning. If we allow this to continue, the entire empire will rise against us."

General Voronov, ever loyal to Igor, nodded in agreement. "We need to act swiftly, Your Highness. If Georgiy continues to gain support, it won't be long before he has enough men to challenge the imperial army."

Igor's eyes darkened. "I won't let it come to that. We strike now, before they can organize. We will crush this rebellion before it even begins."

***

Back in the villa, as Georgiy and his allies were deep in discussion, a messenger arrived, breathless and panicked. He pushed through the door, his face pale with fear.

"Your Highness," the messenger gasped, "Prince Igor is mobilizing the army. They're preparing to move against your supporters in the capital."

The room fell silent, the gravity of the situation sinking in. Amira turned to Georgiy, her expression grim. "It's starting," she said quietly.

Georgiy's heart sank, but there was no time for hesitation. He looked around at his gathered supporters, the weight of leadership heavy on his shoulders. The peaceful path he had once envisioned was slipping away, and the empire was on the brink of civil war.

"We have no choice," Georgiy said finally, his voice steady despite the fear that gripped him. "We need to act now. Gather the people. Tell them we fight for the future of Ata."

Mikhail and the others nodded, moving swiftly to carry out his orders. The rebellion that had been brewing for so long was about to ignite, and Georgiy knew that once the fire started, there would be no turning back.

***

As the sun set over the capital, the streets began to fill with the murmurs of unrest. Word had spread quickly—Prince Igor was preparing to move against those who supported Georgiy's vision, and the people, already on edge after Almosar, were ready to rise.

Scholars, artisans, merchants, and even laborers began to gather in the marketplaces and squares, their voices growing louder with each passing hour. They had seen the brutality of Igor's rule, and they knew that if they didn't act now, they might never have another chance.

Amira stood beside Georgiy as they watched the people rally. "This is it," she said quietly. "The moment we've been waiting for."

Georgiy nodded, but his heart was heavy with the knowledge of what was to come. He had always wanted to lead through peace, through education and progress. But now, as the flames of rebellion grew brighter, he realized that there was no way to avoid the bloodshed that lay ahead.

***

On the other side of the city, Igor's soldiers were already mobilizing. The imperial army, disciplined and ready for battle, marched through the streets, their armor gleaming in the fading light. Igor rode at the head of the column, his face set in a grim mask of determination.

As he neared the center of the capital, where the people had gathered in support of Georgiy, his hand tightened on the hilt of his sword. He had warned his brother, time and time again, that ideals were not enough to hold an empire together. Now, it was time to show him what real power looked like.

Chapter 21

The March of the People

The sun had barely risen when the streets of the capital began to fill with people. A tense energy pulsed through the city as the sounds of marching feet and hushed voices echoed between the towering stone buildings. The common folk—artisans, scholars, merchants, and laborers—gathered in the marketplaces and squares, drawn together by a shared hope for change and the looming threat of violence. It was clear to everyone that the capital was about to become the center of a confrontation that would decide the future of Ata.

Georgiy stood on the balcony of the Great Library, overlooking one of the largest squares where a crowd had already begun to form. The air was thick with anticipation, but also fear. He could see it in their faces—the hope for a better future mingled with the grim realization that bloodshed was inevitable.

Amira stood beside him, her gaze focused on the crowd below. "They're ready for you, Georgiy," she said quietly. "But they're scared. They need to know what they're fighting for."

Georgiy nodded, his expression serious. He had always dreamed of leading through knowledge, of inspiring the people to rise not through violence, but through education and progress. But after the massacre at Almosar and Igor's relentless grip on power, he knew that the time for peaceful change had passed.

"I've spent my life trying to avoid this," Georgiy said softly, his voice tinged with sorrow. "But now there's no choice. If we don't act, Igor will crush them. We must fight—not just for ourselves, but for the future of the empire."

Amira placed a hand on his arm, her eyes steady. "Then you need to give them hope. Show them that this fight is for something greater than just survival. Show them that it's for a new world."

Georgiy took a deep breath, his heart heavy with the weight of the moment. Below, the crowd had grown larger, their voices rising in a chorus of anxious murmurs. The people looked up at him, waiting for their leader to speak.

With a final glance at Amira, Georgiy stepped forward to the edge of the balcony. The crowd quieted as he raised his hand, and for a moment, there was silence. The city seemed to hold its breath.

"People of Ata!" Georgiy called out, his voice ringing through the square. "For too long, we have lived under the weight of fear. For too long, we have been crushed by the burden of taxes, by the cruelty of those who seek only to maintain their power. But today, we say no more!"

A murmur of agreement rippled through the crowd, but Georgiy wasn't finished. He could feel their desperation, their need for direction.

"We are not fighting for revenge," he continued, his voice strong and clear. "We are not fighting out of hatred. We are fighting for the future—our future, and the future of our children. We fight for an empire where knowledge, justice, and compassion guide us, not fear and violence. This is our moment to take back what has been denied to us: our dignity, our rights, and our future!"

The crowd erupted into cheers, their voices rising in unison. Georgiy could see the fire in their eyes now, the determination that had been buried under years of oppression finally coming to the surface.

"We stand together," Georgiy shouted, his voice rising above the roar of the crowd. "And together, we will change the course of history!"

***

Across the city, in the imperial barracks, Prince Igor was preparing for a different kind of speech. He stood before his generals and soldiers, the hard light of dawn filtering through the windows. His expression was cold and resolute, his mind already focused on the battle ahead. The reports of Georgiy's growing influence had reached him, and he knew that the time for decisive action had come.

"This rebellion will end today," Igor said, his voice a low growl. "Georgiy has filled the people's heads with foolish ideas—ideas that will tear this empire apart if we allow them to spread. They think they can defy the crown, that they can rise against the power of the empire. But they are wrong."

General Voronov stepped forward, his face set in a grim mask of loyalty. "Our forces are ready, Your Highness. We can crush them before they have a chance to fully organize."

Igor nodded, his jaw clenched. "Good. We'll march on the city center before they can gather more support. This ends now."

He turned to his soldiers, his eyes burning with the intensity of a man who believed in the righteousness of his cause. "We do this for Ata. We do this to preserve the empire that my father built, the empire that has kept order for generations. We will show them the price of defiance!"

The soldiers, loyal to the core, saluted him in unison. They were ready to follow Igor into battle, ready to crush the rebellion before it could threaten the stability of the empire.

***

As the morning wore on, the streets of the capital grew more crowded. Georgiy's supporters, emboldened by his words, began to march toward the city center. The sound of their footsteps echoed through the narrow alleys, growing louder as more people joined them. Banners were raised, and makeshift weapons were carried by those who had come to fight for their future.

But they were not the only ones on the move.

From the opposite side of the city, Igor's imperial forces were marching as well. Clad in armor and armed with the finest weapons the empire could provide, the soldiers moved in formation, their shields locked and their swords drawn. The streets were eerily quiet as they advanced, the only sound the rhythmic clank of their armor.

The two forces met in the Plaza of the Crescent Moon, the largest square in the capital. On one side stood Georgiy's supporters—men and women who had risen up against the empire's oppression. They were fewer in number than the imperial soldiers, but their resolve was strong. On the other side, Igor's army, disciplined and heavily armed, stood like an impenetrable wall of steel.

For a moment, there was silence.

Georgiy stepped forward, his eyes scanning the faces of the soldiers who stood against him. He knew many of them—men who had once served alongside him in the court, men who had been loyal to the crown. Now, they were enemies.

"We don't have to do this," Georgiy called out, his voice steady. "You are not our enemies. We fight for the same people, the same empire. But we must build a new future together, not through violence, but through understanding."

But Igor's soldiers did not move. They had their orders, and they were loyal to their prince.

From the opposite side of the square, Igor appeared, his face hard and unforgiving. He mounted his horse, riding to the front of his army, his eyes locked on Georgiy.

"You speak of understanding, brother," Igor shouted, his voice dripping with disdain. "But you have led these people to their deaths. You fill their heads with dreams of a world that will never exist, and now they will pay the price for your arrogance."

Georgiy shook his head, his heart heavy. "It's not too late, Igor. We can still stop this. We can find another way."

Igor's eyes narrowed. "There is only one way to deal with rebellion."

He raised his hand, signaling the charge.

***

With a deafening roar, the imperial forces surged forward, their shields raised as they closed the distance between themselves and Georgiy's supporters. The sound of steel clashing against steel filled the square, and in an instant, the peaceful march had turned into a bloody battle.

Georgiy's forces, though determined, were no match for the might of the imperial army. They fought bravely, but they lacked the training and the weapons to hold their ground for long. The square became a sea of chaos, with the imperial soldiers cutting through the ranks of the rebels with brutal efficiency.

Amira, fighting alongside Georgiy, shouted orders to rally the defenders. "Hold the line!" she cried, her voice rising above the din of battle. "Don't let them break through!"

But it was clear that they were being overwhelmed.

Georgiy fought with everything he had, his sword flashing in the sunlight as he defended those around him. He had never wanted this—never wanted to lead his people into violence—but now that the battle had begun, he could not abandon them.

The clash raged on for what felt like hours, but in reality, it was only minutes. The imperial forces, with their superior training and weapons, began to push Georgiy's supporters back, slowly but surely tightening their grip on the square.

As Georgiy fought, he caught sight of Igor, still mounted on his horse, watching the battle with cold detachment. Their eyes met across the chaos, and for a moment, the world seemed to stop.

"This is what it's come to," Georgiy thought, his heart heavy with the weight of what he had tried to prevent. "Brother against brother, fighting for a future that may never come."

But there was no time for hesitation. The battle was far from over, and Georgiy knew that he had to keep fighting—for the people, for the future, for everything he believed in.

Chapter 22

Brothers in Battle

The plaza was a battlefield now, a chaos of shouts, clashing steel, and the cries of the wounded. Georgiy's supporters fought with desperate determination, but they were no match for the disciplined soldiers of the imperial army. Every inch of ground was hard-won, and for every fallen soldier on Igor's side, two of Georgiy's fell. Yet still, the people fought, driven by the hope that Georgiy had sparked in them—a hope for a future free from the iron grip of the empire.

Georgiy himself was in the thick of the fighting, his sword flashing as he parried blows and defended those closest to him. The weight of the battle pressed on him with every swing of his blade. He had never wanted this. He had dreamed of peaceful reform, of changing the empire from within. But now, as he looked around at the blood and death that surrounded him, he wondered if it had all been for nothing.

Amira was beside him, her face streaked with dirt and blood as she fought to keep their lines intact. Her voice rang out above the chaos, shouting orders to rally the defenders, to hold the line as best they could. But it was clear that they were being overwhelmed. The imperial forces, relentless in their advance, were pushing Georgiy's supporters back with every charge.

"We can't hold much longer!" Amira shouted, turning to Georgiy, her eyes filled with concern. "They're too strong!"

Georgiy wiped the sweat from his brow, his breathing heavy. He knew she was right. The imperial soldiers were closing in, their shields locked together as they advanced like an unstoppable wave. They were outnumbered, outmatched, and running out of time.

But as Georgiy scanned the battlefield, his gaze fell on his brother.

Igor stood on the far side of the square, watching the battle unfold with cold detachment. He hadn't yet joined the fray, content to let his soldiers do the fighting for him. But Georgiy knew that the true battle wouldn't be fought with swords and shields. It would be fought between the two of them—brother against brother, each fighting for the soul of the empire.

"This has to end," Georgiy muttered to himself, his mind racing. "It can't go on like this."

Without hesitation, Georgiy pushed his way through the melee, his eyes locked on Igor. He could feel Amira calling after him, but her voice was lost in the din of battle. Georgiy knew what he had to do. If there was any chance of saving the people, of stopping the slaughter, he would have to confront Igor directly.

✳✳✳

As Georgiy made his way across the battlefield, the fighting seemed to blur around him. His focus narrowed until there was only Igor—the brother who had once fought beside him, but who now stood as his greatest enemy. The brother who had chosen strength and fear over the ideals of justice and knowledge.

Igor saw him coming. Their eyes met across the square, and for a moment, it was as if the rest of the world faded away. The sounds of battle seemed to dim, leaving only the two of them, locked in a moment that had been building for years.

Igor dismounted from his horse, handing the reins to one of his soldiers. His face was hard, unreadable, as he drew his sword and stepped forward to meet Georgiy.

When they finally stood face to face, the weight of their history hung between them—years of shared struggles, of competing visions for the future of Ata. And now, everything had come to this.

"You shouldn't have come here, Georgiy," Igor said, his voice cold and measured. "You've led these people to their deaths."

Georgiy's heart pounded in his chest, but he refused to let fear cloud his resolve. "I didn't lead them to this, Igor. You did. Your cruelty, your fear—this is what drove them to rise. They're not fighting for me; they're fighting for their future. A future you're trying to take from them."

Igor's eyes flashed with anger. "The future you're promising them doesn't exist. It's a fantasy, Georgiy. A world where people rule themselves? Where knowledge alone is enough to hold an empire together? That's not how the world works. Power is the only thing that keeps the empire strong. Without it, we fall into chaos."

"The empire is already falling apart!" Georgiy shot back, his voice rising. "Look around you! The people are suffering. They're tired of living in fear. They want something better, something real. But all you offer them is more bloodshed!"

Igor stepped closer, his grip tightening on his sword. "Bloodshed is the only thing they understand. You can't build a future on dreams, brother. You build it with strength. With control."

For a moment, neither of them moved. The tension between them crackled like a live wire, the clash of their ideologies hanging in the air. But Georgiy knew that words alone wouldn't be enough to end this. His brother was too far gone, too entrenched in his belief that force was the only way to rule. There was no reasoning with him.

There was only one way this would end.

"I won't let you destroy this empire," Georgiy said quietly, his voice filled with determination. "I won't let you kill the future."

Igor's eyes narrowed, his lips curling into a grim smile. "Then come and stop me."

***

In an instant, the tension snapped, and the two brothers lunged at each other, swords clashing with a deafening ring. The world around them seemed to fade into the background as they fought—two opposing forces, locked in a battle not just of skill, but of will.

Georgiy fought with a desperation he hadn't felt before. Every swing of his sword was filled with the weight of his beliefs, his dreams for a better Ata. But Igor was relentless, his strikes powerful and precise, driven by his unwavering belief in the necessity of control.

The duel was brutal and fast, each brother pushing the other to their limits. Their swords clanged and sparked as they moved across the battlefield, the chaos of the larger fight swirling around them.

Igor was the better fighter—Georgiy had always known that. His brother had spent years in the military, leading campaigns and crushing rebellions. Georgiy, on the other hand, had devoted his life to learning, to understanding the world in a different way. But now, in this moment, it all came down to this fight.

Blow after blow, they matched each other's attacks, neither willing to give an inch. But Georgiy could feel his strength waning. Igor's strikes were coming faster, more aggressive, and Georgiy knew that he couldn't keep up much longer.

With a final, powerful strike, Igor knocked Georgiy's sword from his hand, sending it clattering across the cobblestones. Georgiy stumbled back, his chest heaving as he struggled to catch his breath.

Igor advanced, his sword raised, his face set in grim determination. "It's over, Georgiy," he said quietly, his voice almost sad. "You've lost."

Georgiy looked up at his brother, his heart heavy with the weight of failure. He had tried to save the empire, to give the people hope for a better future. But now, as he stood unarmed before Igor, he realized that his dream might die here, in this blood-soaked square.

But then, something shifted.

The sound of footsteps, of voices rising in unison, filled the square. Georgiy looked past his brother and saw them—his supporters, the people of Ata, marching toward them. Despite the chaos, despite the violence, they were still there, still fighting. They believed in him. They believed in the future he had promised them.

Georgiy's heart swelled with renewed hope.

"It's not over," he said softly, his voice filled with quiet defiance. "Not yet."

Igor hesitated, his eyes narrowing as he looked at the crowd gathering behind Georgiy. He could see it now—the strength of the people, their resolve. And for the first time, doubt flickered across his face.

Before he could react, a sharp whistle cut through the air, and an arrow flew past Igor's shoulder, embedding itself in the ground between them. Igor turned, startled, just as a surge of Georgiy's supporters pushed forward, overwhelming the imperial soldiers.

The tide of the battle was shifting.

***

Igor cursed under his breath, his eyes flashing with fury. He looked back at Georgiy, his expression filled with anger and frustration.

"This isn't over, brother," Igor snarled, backing away, his sword still drawn. "You may have won today, but the empire will never be yours."

With that, he turned and signaled his soldiers to retreat. The imperial forces, seeing their leader pull back, began to fall back as well, leaving the battlefield to Georgiy and his supporters.

Georgiy watched as Igor disappeared into the chaos, his heart pounding. The battle had been won—for now—but he knew this was only the beginning. The empire was still fractured, still teetering on the edge of collapse. There would be more fighting, more bloodshed before the future he dreamed of could be realized.

But for the first time, he saw hope.

The people of Ata were with him. And as long as they stood together, he knew that the future was still within reach.

Georgiy lowered his sword, his heart still racing, but now filled with a different kind of energy—hope. The people who had fought by his side had shown resilience, and despite the odds, they had pushed Igor back. As the dust settled over the battlefield, a sense of unity began to grow among his supporters.

Amira approached him, wiping the sweat and dirt from her face, her eyes filled with cautious optimism. "We did it," she said, her voice a mix of relief and concern. "But this is just the beginning, isn't it?"

Georgiy nodded, his gaze still fixed on the horizon where Igor had disappeared. "Yes. Igor will be back, and he'll come with more men, more force. He won't accept this defeat. Not now, not ever."

Amira placed a hand on his arm, her grip strong. "Then we need to prepare. We need to strengthen our alliances, rally more of the provinces to our cause. Igor can't win if the people refuse to fight for him."

Georgiy turned to her, the fire of determination rekindled in his eyes. "We will. This battle has shown that the people are ready for change, ready to stand against oppression. But we need more than just courage—we need strategy, we need support. We need to give the people of Ata something worth fighting for."

"And we will," Amira replied. "The empire is changing, and for the first time, it feels like the people are leading that change."

Georgiy smiled, though it was tinged with sadness. "I never wanted this war, but it's here now. And if we're to win, we have to fight not just with swords, but with ideas—with the vision of the future we want to build."

Amira nodded, understanding the weight of his words. "And we will. Together."

As they stood side by side, looking out over the aftermath of the battle, Georgiy knew that the road ahead would be long and difficult. But for the first time since the conflict with his brother had begun, he believed that a better future for Ata was possible.

With his people behind him and the resolve to carry on, Georgiy knew that the fight was far from over—but the flame of hope had been lit, and it was now up to him to keep it burning.

Chapter 23
The Aftermath of the Battle

The plaza was eerily quiet in the wake of the retreat. The din of battle had given way to a tense silence, broken only by the groans of the wounded and the distant sound of Igor's forces falling back through the narrow streets. Georgiy stood amidst the rubble and blood, his breath coming in ragged gasps, his heart still pounding from the confrontation with his brother. Around him, his supporters—those who had survived the battle—began to regroup, helping the injured and tending to the fallen.

Amira appeared at his side, her face a mixture of relief and worry. She had been watching the duel, her heart in her throat as Georgiy fought against Igor, and she knew how close the battle had come to ending in tragedy.

"You did it," she said quietly, her voice filled with cautious hope. "You held the line. We've won."

Georgiy looked around at the faces of the people who had followed him into this fight. Some were injured, others exhausted, but they were still standing. For now, they had driven Igor's forces back, but the victory felt hollow. The square was littered with the bodies of the dead, both imperial soldiers and common folk. The cost of this battle had been high, and the fight for Ata was far from over.

"It doesn't feel like a victory," Georgiy said, his voice thick with emotion. "Too many people died today. And Igor—he'll be back. He won't stop until he crushes us completely."

Amira placed a hand on his arm, her grip firm. "We knew this would be a long fight. But today, you showed the people that they don't have to live in fear anymore. You showed them that they can stand up to Igor and the empire. That's a victory."

Georgiy sighed, the weight of leadership pressing down on him like never before. "I didn't want it to come to this. I never wanted to lead a rebellion. But now that we've started, there's no going back."

Amira nodded, her gaze steady. "You've given them hope, Georgiy. That's something Igor can never take away. But we need to act quickly. The people are with you now, but if Igor regroups and attacks again, we may not survive another battle like this."

Georgiy ran a hand through his hair, his mind racing. "We need to gather more support—reach out to the provinces, rally the people outside the capital. If we're going to stand a chance against Igor, we need more than just the city. We need the whole empire."

***

As Igor's forces retreated through the streets of the capital, the prince seethed with anger. His jaw clenched tightly, and his grip on his sword was so tight his knuckles turned white. The sight of Georgiy standing victorious in the plaza burned in his mind. This wasn't how it was supposed to go. He had been certain of his victory, certain that his brother's rebellion would be crushed with a single decisive strike.

"He thinks he's won," Igor muttered under his breath as his generals rode alongside him. "But this is only the beginning."

General Voronov, ever loyal, looked to Igor with concern. "What are our next steps, Your Highness? The rebels are gaining strength. If we don't act quickly, they could seize more cities."

Igor's face hardened as he turned to his general. "We regroup. I won't make the mistake of underestimating Georgiy again. He's a fool, but he's dangerous. We'll fortify our position, call for reinforcements from the northern provinces. And when we're ready, we'll crush him and his supporters once and for all."

Voronov nodded, though even he seemed unsettled by the events of the day. "And what about the nobles? Some of them are beginning to waver. They're seeing Georgiy's rise in power as a threat—but also as an opportunity."

Igor's eyes flashed with fury. "Any noble who dares to side with Georgiy will meet the same fate as the rebels. I won't tolerate dissent within the ranks. If they want to test me, they'll regret it."

But beneath Igor's fury, a sliver of doubt had taken root. The people had rallied to Georgiy's side, and the fight had not gone as planned. Igor had thought his brother weak, too idealistic to be a threat. But now, after seeing Georgiy lead his people into battle, he realized that his brother's ideals had power—power that could threaten his rule.

"I won't let him win," Igor thought darkly, his resolve hardening. "This is my empire. And I will stop at nothing to keep it."

***

Night had fallen over the capital, casting long shadows over the city that had become a battlefield. In the aftermath of the battle, Georgiy's supporters had gathered in a makeshift camp at the edge of the plaza. Fires flickered in the night as they tended to the wounded and discussed their next steps.

Georgiy sat with Amira and his closest allies—Lord Mikhail, Lady Serafina, and a handful of others who had stood by him since the beginning. The exhaustion of the day weighed heavily on all of them, but they knew there was no time to rest. The empire was still on the brink of collapse, and they had to act quickly if they wanted to keep the momentum from the day's victory.

"Igor will be back," Georgiy said, his voice quiet but firm. "We can't wait for him to attack again. We need to move first, while we still have the upper hand."

Mikhail, who had proven himself a skilled strategist, nodded in agreement. "The provinces are key. If we can rally support outside the capital, we can force Igor to spread his forces thin. He'll be fighting on multiple fronts, and that will give us a chance to strike at the heart of his power."

Lady Serafina, though weary, spoke up. "The nobles are divided. Some of them still support Igor, but there are many who are beginning to see Georgiy's vision as the future. We need to secure their loyalty—if we can get the nobles on our side, we'll have the resources and influence to challenge Igor directly."

Georgiy leaned back, his mind racing. The path ahead was fraught with danger, but for the first time, he felt a glimmer of hope. The people had risen, and the nobles were beginning to waver. If he could unite them, if he could build a coalition of those who believed in his vision, he might just have a chance to bring real change to Ata.

But there was still the question of his father—the king who had been silent throughout the conflict, watching as his sons tore the empire apart.

"We need to reach the king," Georgiy said suddenly, his gaze focused. "He's the only one who can stop this before it spirals out of control. If I can convince him to side with us, to embrace reform, then maybe—just maybe—we can avoid a full-scale civil war."

Amira looked at him, her expression thoughtful. "It's a risk, Georgiy. The king has always favored Igor. And he's grown weaker in recent months. If you confront him now, you could be walking into a trap."

Georgiy nodded, acknowledging the danger. "I know. But we have no choice. If we don't act soon, Igor will regroup, and this city will drown in blood. I have to try. For the sake of the people, for the future of the empire, I have to try."

***

The next morning, Georgiy prepared to leave the camp and make his way to the royal palace. The city was still tense, with imperial soldiers patrolling the streets, but Georgiy's supporters were keeping watch. It was a dangerous mission—there was no guarantee that the king would even agree to see him, and if Igor learned of his plan, it could mean certain death.

Amira stood with Georgiy as he mounted his horse, her face filled with concern. "Are you sure about this?" she asked, her voice quiet. "Igor won't let you go without a fight if he finds out."

Georgiy met her gaze, his eyes steady. "I have to try, Amira. If I can convince our father to listen, we can end this before it gets worse. If not..." He trailed off, the weight of the risk hanging between them.

Amira placed a hand on his arm. "Then be careful. We need you. The people need you."

Georgiy gave her a small, determined smile. "I'll be back. And when I return, we'll take the next step together."

With that, he spurred his horse forward, heading toward the royal palace—toward the father who had watched in silence as his sons led the empire to the brink of destruction.

Chapter 23

Civil Unrest

The winds of rebellion carried fast across Ata, faster than anyone in the capital could have anticipated. News of Georgiy's resistance, his battle against the imperial army, and the growing support for his vision spread to the farthest reaches of the empire. In the provinces, where the common people had long been burdened by crippling taxes and persistent food shortages, the flame of unrest began to flicker. Farmers, artisans, and laborers, already struggling under the weight of imperial demands, saw Georgiy's defiance as a sign that change was possible.

Small uprisings began to break out in villages and towns that had once been quiet. In the southern provinces, long known for their agricultural wealth but crushed by taxation, peasants rose up against local governors. In the west, miners who toiled in gold and silver mines took up arms, refusing to send their precious resources to the capital. Everywhere, the whispers of rebellion grew louder, and the name "Georgiy" became a rallying cry for those who had suffered in silence for too long.

The ideals of education, justice, and progress that Georgiy had championed during his public speeches before the battle resonated deeply with the people. They began to view his fight not just as a personal rebellion against his brother Igor, but as a movement for a new kind of empire—one where knowledge and equality ruled over fear and power.

***

Though he had narrowly escaped capture in the capital and was in hiding, Georgiy continued to spread his message. He knew that the battle for Ata was not won through violence alone, but through ideas. Using a network of loyal supporters, Georgiy sent letters and proclamations to the provinces, urging the people not to fall into a cycle of revenge and hatred. Instead, he asked them to fight for a future that would benefit everyone in the empire—rich and poor, noble and commoner alike.

In his letters, Georgiy wrote:

"We fight not for vengeance, but for the future of our children and for the soul of Ata. We must not tear down this empire; we must rebuild it from within. Education, justice, and science will guide us, and through these, we will create a future where no one is left behind. Together, we are stronger than the chains of fear that have held us for so long."

Georgiy's supporters began to organize under the name Za Lyubov—"For Love"—echoing the love for knowledge and humanity that lay at the heart of his vision. They saw themselves not as revolutionaries, but as reformers, fighting to create an empire where the pursuit of knowledge and progress would free them from the oppression of the past.

Leaders began to emerge within the Za Lyubov movement. In the eastern provinces, scholars took the lead, calling for the establishment of schools where the poor could learn the sciences, medicine, and technology. In the south, farmers demanded a redistribution of land and resources, while in the cities, artisans and merchants organized guilds to protect their interests and push for economic reform. These leaders coordinated efforts, organizing the movement into something more formal, with the ultimate goal of uniting the empire under Georgiy's vision.

***

While the provinces stirred with new hope, Igor seethed in the capital. The defeat he had suffered at the hands of his brother and the rebellion that followed it had wounded his pride and his authority. Worse, the empire that had always been so firmly under his control was beginning to slip through his fingers. To Igor, the unrest in the provinces was not about justice or education; it was treason, pure and simple.

Determined to crush the rebellion before it could gain more traction, Igor ordered a brutal crackdown on the uprisings. He dispatched imperial forces to the provinces, commanding them to restore order with an iron fist. The soldiers, loyal to Igor and emboldened by his fury, swept through villages and towns with ruthless efficiency. They raided homes, arrested suspected rebels, and burned any village that was rumored to harbor supporters of Georgiy. Those who defied the empire were executed publicly, their bodies left as a grim reminder of the price of rebellion.

But the crackdown, rather than quelling the unrest, only inflamed it. For every rebel that Igor's forces executed, ten more rose in their place. The brutality of the imperial army deepened the people's hatred for the regime. Rather than retreating in fear, the people became more determined to stand up to the empire. They saw themselves as fighting not just for survival, but for the future that Georgiy had promised them—a future where they would no longer live in fear.

In cities and villages across Ata, the cry of "Za Lyubov!" grew louder, and the movement gained strength with each passing day. The people, once divided by geography and class, were united by the hope of a new empire—an empire of justice, knowledge, and equality. And as the unrest spread, it became clear that the fight for Ata had only just begun.

Chapter 24
The Elites Push Back

As unrest swept through the provinces, the noble class in the capital grew increasingly anxious. The rebellion had been contained—for now—but the embers of discontent continued to smolder. The nobles had watched with growing horror as Georgiy's ideas took root in the minds of the common people. The concept of education for all, the redistribution of wealth, and a future where the elites no longer ruled by birthright threatened everything they had built their lives around. And worse still, the uprisings had given Georgiy's movement momentum.

In the grand chambers of the palace, the nobles met in secret councils, debating how best to preserve their power. Lord Kazimir, one of the oldest and most influential nobles, spoke first.

"We've let this go on for too long," he said, his voice hard with anger. "Georgiy's rebellion was a failure, yes, but his ideas live on. And those ideas are far more dangerous than any army he could ever muster."

The younger nobles in the room exchanged uneasy glances. Many of them had sympathized with Georgiy's vision, at least in the beginning. The idea of reform had seemed reasonable at first—a way to keep the empire strong by making small concessions. But now, with the provinces on the verge of revolt and Igor's imperial forces stretched thin, it was clear that Georgiy's movement could no longer be dismissed as a minor annoyance.

"If we don't act now," Kazimir continued, "we will lose control of this empire. Georgiy's ideals are spreading, and soon, even the people here in the capital will rise up. We must crush this movement before it destroys everything we have worked for."

***

While the nobles conspired, King Sergey remained isolated in his chambers. His once-vigorous frame was now frail, and his health had deteriorated significantly. He had tried to stay above the conflict between his sons, hoping that they would find a way to reconcile without tearing the empire apart. But now, with the unrest in the provinces and the growing pressure from the nobles, he knew that he could no longer remain neutral.

As he sat in his private study, the weight of the crown pressed heavily on him. Georgiy's ideals had merit—Sergey knew that. The empire needed to change if it was to survive. But the way Georgiy had gone about it—through rebellion, through open defiance—had fractured the very foundation of the empire. And Igor, though loyal and strong, was too harsh, too rigid in his belief that only fear and control could keep the people in line.

Sergey sighed, his hands trembling as he held a letter from one of the southern provinces, begging for relief from the taxes and military oppression. His heart ached for his people, but his mind was clouded by the reality of the political situation. The nobles were demanding action, and if he didn't act, they might turn against him. But siding with Igor meant more brutality, more bloodshed—and siding with Georgiy meant risking the stability of the entire empire.

The king's thoughts were interrupted by a soft knock on the door. His personal advisor, Vasil, entered, his face drawn with concern.

"Your Majesty," Vasil began, his voice low, "the nobles are demanding a decision. They want you to take a definitive stance on the rebellion and the unrest. If you do not act soon, they fear the empire will fall into chaos."

Sergey closed his eyes, the pressure mounting. "And if I side with Georgiy? What then?"

Vasil hesitated. "Then the nobles will likely withdraw their support. They see Georgiy's ideals as a threat to their power. Some are already aligning themselves with Prince Igor, hoping to ensure their position if the conflict escalates."

The king's heart sank. He knew what this meant—if he did not act, the nobles would turn to Igor, and the empire would become a dictatorship ruled by fear. If he sided with Georgiy, the fragile stability that had kept the empire together would collapse.

***

Later that evening, King Sergey summoned a council of the most powerful nobles in the empire. The room was tense, the air thick with anticipation as the nobles gathered around the long, gilded table. Lord Kazimir sat at the head, flanked by other members of the conservative elite, while the younger, more progressive nobles took their places at the opposite end.

The conversation began cordially, but it wasn't long before the nobles presented their ultimatum. "Your Majesty," Kazimir said, his voice firm but respectful, "the time has come for you to choose. Georgiy's rebellion was an act of treason, and his followers are sowing chaos in the provinces. If you do not take decisive action to suppress this movement, the empire will fall."

Several of the younger nobles, including Lady Serafina, exchanged uneasy glances. They had no love for Igor's methods, but they also feared the consequences of further unrest. Still, they were hesitant to see Georgiy's movement crushed entirely.

"There must be another way," Serafina interjected, her voice soft but clear. "Georgiy's ideals have merit. The people are suffering. If we address their grievances, we might avoid further bloodshed."

Kazimir scoffed, his expression hardening. "Address their grievances? By what—giving them power? Opening schools for peasants? Redistributing wealth? This is not the empire our ancestors built. This is madness."

Sergey, seated at the head of the table, listened silently as the debate raged on. His mind swirled with doubt and uncertainty. He knew that siding with the nobles and Igor would bring short-term stability, but it would come at a terrible cost—the cost of the people's trust, their hope for a better future. And yet, siding with Georgiy could lead to chaos, perhaps even the collapse of the empire itself.

Finally, Kazimir turned to the king, his eyes cold and determined. "Your Majesty, if you do not act now—if you do not order the suppression of this movement—the nobles will have no choice but to act without you."

The ultimatum hung in the air, heavy and foreboding. Sergey felt the weight of his crown pressing down on him more than ever before.

"I will consider your counsel," he said quietly, dismissing the council with a wave of his hand. The nobles left the room, but the king remained seated, his heart heavy with the impossible decision before him.

Chapter 25
Georgiy's Dilemma

The Za Lyubov movement, which had begun with hope and a shared vision for the future, was beginning to fracture. In the weeks following the uprisings across Ata, small victories in the provinces had emboldened some of Georgiy's supporters. But as the movement grew, so did the divisions within it. Different factions emerged, each with their own interpretation of what the movement should be, and how they should move forward.

In the southern provinces, where the rebellion was strongest, the leaders of the movement pushed for a more aggressive approach. They had tasted victory, however small, and they believed the time was ripe for a full-scale revolution. The people were ready, they argued, and the imperial forces were overstretched. If they struck now, they could seize control of more territories and force the empire into submission.

In the cities, however, the scholars and artisans who had rallied behind Georgiy's message of reform were more cautious. They feared that escalating the conflict would only lead to more bloodshed and that the ideals of education, knowledge, and progress would be lost in the violence. They wanted to focus on building schools, redistributing resources, and slowly gaining the people's trust through peaceful means.

Georgiy, still recovering from the battles he had fought in the capital, found himself caught between these two factions. He had always believed in peaceful reform, in the power of ideas to change the world. But now, as the empire spiraled deeper into chaos, he could feel the growing desperation among his followers. He knew that if he didn't make a decision soon, the movement could splinter beyond repair.

***

One evening, Georgiy sat in a dimly lit chamber in the heart of the southern provinces, staring at a map of the empire. His mind was racing, torn between the path of peaceful reform he had always envisioned and the reality of the escalating conflict. Across the table sat Amira, his closest confidante and the voice of reason that had guided him throughout the struggle.

"You've been quiet," Amira said, her sharp eyes studying him. "What's going through your mind?"

Georgiy sighed, leaning back in his chair. "I don't know what to do, Amira. I've always believed that we could change this empire without destroying it. But now... now I'm not so sure. The people are angry. They're ready to fight, and if I don't lead them, they'll follow someone else. But if we push too hard, we risk losing everything—our ideals, our vision for the future. How can I reconcile that?"

Amira leaned forward, her gaze intense. "You have to understand something, Georgiy. You've inspired these people. They believe in you, in your vision for a better world. But they're also scared. They've seen what Igor is capable of, and they know that if they don't act, they'll be crushed. You can't ask them to wait forever. If you don't give them a way forward, they'll start looking for answers elsewhere."

Georgiy frowned, rubbing his temples. "I don't want to lead them into more violence."

"Then don't," Amira replied firmly. "But you have to give them something. You can't just preach ideals while the empire burns. The people are ready to act, and you need to lead them. That doesn't mean abandoning your vision. It means adapting, finding a way to move forward without losing what you stand for."

Her words hung in the air, heavy with truth. Georgiy knew she was right, but the decision weighed on him like a mountain. He had come so far, yet the path ahead seemed more uncertain than ever.

***

As Georgiy wrestled with his inner turmoil, a group of rebel leaders from the southern provinces arrived at his camp. They had been instrumental in leading the uprisings in their regions, and now they sought Georgiy's guidance on the next steps. But they had come with an ultimatum of their own.

The leader of the group, Dmitri, a hardened farmer who had risen to prominence through his leadership in the rebellion, approached Georgiy with urgency in his voice. "Prince Georgiy," Dmitri began, "the people in the south are ready to follow you, but we need your leadership. We can't wait any longer. The empire is weak, and if we strike now, we can force Igor's hand. The time for peaceful reform has passed."

Georgiy met Dmitri's gaze, his expression grim. "I understand the urgency, Dmitri, but I don't want to lead these people into a war that will cost more lives than we can afford. I still believe we can change things without tearing the empire apart."

Dmitri shook his head, frustration flashing in his eyes. "With all due respect, Your Highness, the empire is already falling apart. You've seen what Igor has done. His forces are burning villages, executing our people. We're not asking for violence, but if we don't defend ourselves, we'll be crushed. The people need more than words now. They need action."

The other leaders murmured in agreement. "We're ready to follow you, Dmitri continued, "but you need to lead us. If you don't, someone else will—and they might not share your vision for the future."

Georgiy felt the weight of their words. He looked at Amira, who watched silently, her expression unreadable. She had warned him that this moment was coming, that he would have to choose between his ideals and the reality of the situation.

***

That night, Georgiy stood on a hill overlooking the camp, the soft glow of campfires flickering in the distance. He watched as his followers, many of them simple farmers, artisans, and workers, prepared for what might be their last stand against the empire. These were the people he had sworn to protect, the people who had believed in his vision of a better future. And now, they were depending on him to lead them through the storm.

Amira joined him, her footsteps soft on the grass. "Have you made your decision?" she asked quietly.

Georgiy nodded, though his heart was heavy. "I have."

"And?"

"I'll lead them," Georgiy said, his voice firm. "But I won't lead them into war for the sake of war. I'll lead them to defend themselves, to protect the future we're trying to build. If it comes to fighting, so be it. But we'll do it on our terms, not Igor's."

Amira smiled faintly, her eyes filled with both pride and sorrow. "You've always known the right path, Georgiy. Now, you just need to walk it."

Georgiy took a deep breath, feeling the weight of his decision settle over him. The path ahead was uncertain, and he knew that there would be bloodshed before peace could be achieved. But he also knew that this was his moment—his chance to lead his people toward the future they all dreamed of.

And so, as the dawn broke over the horizon, Georgiy made his way back to the camp, ready to take up the mantle of leadership once again. The time for action had come.

Chapter 26
Revolutionary Leadership

With his resolve solidified, Georgiy's first act as leader was to launch a bold, symbolic gesture that would both defy the empire and inspire his followers. He announced the opening of the first Space School Academy in the heart of one of the rebellious southern provinces. This act, while seemingly peaceful, was an open challenge to the empire's authority. The academy was not just a place for education; it was a beacon of what the future could be—a future where knowledge, science, and progress guided the people of Ata, not fear and oppression.

The school welcomed students from all classes—noble and common alike—and promised to teach subjects that had long been reserved for the elites: astronomy, medicine, engineering, and philosophy. For the people of Ata, the academy represented a new hope, a tangible example of the world Georgiy was fighting to create.

As the school doors opened, the people of the province gathered in the square outside, their faces filled with awe and pride. Parents brought their children, hoping they would be among the first to attend. Scholars and teachers, many of whom had been silent supporters of Georgiy's cause, came forward to offer their services.

"This is the future," Georgiy declared to the gathered crowd, standing before the academy's gates. "A future where every child, no matter their birth, can learn, grow, and contribute to the greatness of our empire. This is what we fight for—not just the end of oppression, but the beginning of something new. Today, we plant the seeds of tomorrow's leaders, doctors, and scientists. And with your support, this will be just the first of many schools to come."

The crowd erupted into cheers, their voices carrying hope across the square. But Georgiy knew that this moment of triumph was fleeting. The imperial forces would not stand for such a direct challenge. He had lit the spark, but now the flame would need to be defended.

***

The opening of the academy sent shockwaves throughout Ata. Word of Georgiy's defiance spread quickly, and as expected, it reached the ears of Prince Igor. The message was clear: Georgiy was not only refusing to back down, but he was also building the future he envisioned right under the empire's nose. To Igor, this was not just rebellion; it was treason.

Igor's fury was swift. He summoned his most loyal generals and ordered them to prepare a force to march on the province where the academy had been established. "Destroy it," Igor commanded, his voice cold and resolute. "Burn it to the ground. Let the people see what happens when they defy the empire."

Imperial soldiers marched south, prepared to crush the academy and the ideals it represented. Meanwhile, in the provinces, the Za Lyubov movement began to arm itself in preparation for the inevitable clash. Dmitri and the other rebel leaders had anticipated this response, and they rallied their forces to defend the academy at all costs.

***

As the imperial army closed in, the weight of Georgiy's decision became clear. He had chosen to stand, to defend the academy and the ideals it represented, even if it meant leading his followers into battle. The peaceful revolution he had once envisioned was slipping further away, replaced by the harsh reality of war.

In the days leading up to the confrontation, Georgiy addressed his people, his voice steady but filled with the gravity of the situation.

"I never wanted this," he said to a gathering of his followers. "I never wanted to lead us into war. But the empire has left us no choice. We fight not for violence, but to defend the future we want to build. If we don't stand together now, if we don't protect this academy and what it represents, then we lose more than just a building—we lose hope. We lose the chance to shape our destiny."

His words resonated with the people. They knew the stakes were high, and though many of them were farmers, artisans, and scholars—not soldiers—they were willing to fight for what Georgiy had inspired in them. For the first time in their lives, they felt like they had a say in the future of Ata. And they weren't about to let that go.

***

The day of the confrontation arrived quickly. Imperial forces descended on the province, their banners flying high as they marched toward the academy. The sight of the imperial army struck fear into the hearts of many, but Georgiy's forces, though smaller and less experienced, were prepared to defend what they had built.

Georgiy, standing at the front of his forces, looked out across the battlefield. He could see the imperial soldiers forming their lines, their armor gleaming in the morning light. He knew this was more than just a battle for the academy—this was a battle for the soul of Ata.

Dmitri stood beside him, a grim expression on his face. "They outnumber us, but we have something they don't," Dmitri said. "We have purpose. And we have you."

Georgiy nodded, though his heart was heavy. He knew that many of the people who stood with him today would not survive. But this was their stand. If they won, the empire would have no choice but to acknowledge the power of the people. If they lost... well, Georgiy refused to think of that outcome.

The battle began with a thunderous roar as the imperial forces charged forward. The defenders of the academy, armed with whatever they could find—makeshift weapons, farm tools, and stolen swords—met them with fierce resistance. The clash of steel and the cries of battle filled the air as the two sides fought for control of the academy.

Georgiy fought alongside his people, his sword flashing as he parried blows and defended those around him. He had never been a soldier, but in this moment, he felt the weight of every life that had been lost in the fight for a better future. Each swing of his sword was a promise to his people: that he would not abandon them, that he would fight for their right to learn, to grow, to live without fear.

***

As the battle raged on, it became clear that the imperial forces, though larger and better equipped, were unprepared for the ferocity of the resistance. The defenders fought with everything they had, fueled by their belief in Georgiy's vision. And as the imperial lines began to falter, hope surged through the hearts of the rebels.

In a decisive moment, Georgiy and Dmitri led a charge that broke through the imperial ranks, sending the soldiers into disarray. The tide of the battle shifted, and soon the imperial forces were retreating, their once-imposing army now in full flight.

As the dust settled and the battlefield grew quiet, Georgiy stood before the academy, battered but victorious. The people cheered, their voices ringing out across the province. They had won—not just the battle, but the right to believe in a future where they could shape their own destiny.

But Georgiy knew this was only the beginning.

***

As night fell, Georgiy gathered his closest advisors, including Dmitri and Amira, to discuss the next steps. The victory had given them momentum, but it had also made them an even greater target for the empire. Igor would not take this defeat lightly, and the full force of the imperial army would soon come crashing down on them.

"We've won today," Georgiy said, his voice calm but resolute. "But we must be ready for what comes next. Igor will strike again, and when he does, we need to be stronger, more organized. We need to spread our message further, to rally more of the provinces to our cause. This battle is over, but the war has just begun."

Amira nodded, her expression thoughtful. "We need more than just fighters, Georgiy. We need thinkers, strategists, and diplomats. If we're going to win, we need to build alliances—not just with the people, but with those in power who are willing to see the value of your vision."

Georgiy agreed, knowing that the path forward would require not just strength, but wisdom. The victory had proven that his movement could stand against the empire, but now they needed to grow, to evolve, if they were to survive the next confrontation.

Chapter 27

The Space Revolution

In the weeks following the battle at the academy, uprisings erupted across Ata. From the mines of the western provinces to the fertile farmlands of the south, Georgiy's supporters rallied to his cause. Farmers refused to send their harvests to the capital, artisans and scholars formed alliances to protect their communities, and local militias were organized to resist the empire's forces.

Each new rebellion was different, shaped by the needs and grievances of the people in that region. In the cities, the rebellion was led by scholars and artisans who embraced Georgiy's vision of universal education. They began to open underground schools, teaching the sciences, mathematics, and philosophy to anyone who would listen. These schools became centers of learning, but also hubs for organizing resistance against the empire.

In the countryside, the rebellion was more practical. Farmers and laborers, long oppressed by imperial taxes, rose up to defend their land and their families. They destroyed imperial grain stores, disrupted trade routes, and took over local garrisons. The countryside became a patchwork of rebel-controlled territories, where imperial authority held little sway.

Georgiy's ideals of education, equality, and justice became the rallying cry for the revolution. People who had once lived in fear now believed they had a stake in the future of the empire. And as the rebellion spread, so did Georgiy's message: the revolution was not just about overthrowing the old order—it was about building a new one.

***

As the revolution spread, so too did Igor's response. The defeat at the academy had been a humiliation, and Igor vowed that it would not happen again. He unleashed the full might of the imperial army, ordering his generals to crush the uprisings with overwhelming force. His tactics were brutal and uncompromising. He believed that only through fear and violence could the empire be held together.

Imperial forces descended upon rebel-held territories like a storm. Villages were razed, and entire families were executed as a warning to others who might defy the empire. In the cities, anyone suspected of harboring rebels or sympathizing with the revolution was arrested, tortured, or killed. Imperial soldiers patrolled the streets, imposing curfews and enforcing martial law.

But Igor's brutality, rather than quelling the rebellion, only fueled it further. The people of Ata, already weary of years of oppression, became even more determined to resist. For every rebel that the empire executed, ten more rose up in their place. The more Igor tried to tighten his grip on the empire, the more it slipped through his fingers.

In secret meetings, rebel leaders debated how to respond. Some argued for more aggressive tactics, urging Georgiy to launch a full-scale assault on the capital. Others, particularly the scholars and teachers, insisted that the revolution should remain focused on education and progress, even in the face of violence.

***

For Georgiy, these were the darkest days of the revolution. While the victories in the provinces gave him hope, the brutality of Igor's response weighed heavily on him. He had always believed in a peaceful path to reform, but now he found himself leading an armed rebellion, responsible for the lives of thousands. Each new battle, each report of atrocities committed by imperial forces, chipped away at his idealism.

He began to question his own decisions. Was he leading his people down a path that would only bring more suffering? Or was this the only way to achieve the future he had dreamed of for so long?

Late one night, as Georgiy poured over reports of the growing conflict, Amira entered his tent. She had been his closest advisor since the beginning, and she could see the toll that the revolution was taking on him.

"You look tired," she said, sitting across from him. "You've barely slept in days."

Georgiy sighed, rubbing his eyes. "There's too much at stake, Amira. Every day, more people join the cause, and every day, more lives are lost. I didn't want this war, but I don't see any other way forward."

Amira studied him for a moment before speaking. "This was never going to be easy, Georgiy. But you need to remember why we're fighting. It's not just about survival—it's about creating something better. The people believe in you, in your vision for the future. That's why they fight. Don't lose sight of that."

Georgiy nodded, though the weight of leadership still pressed down on him. "I won't. But sometimes, it feels like the ideals we're fighting for are slipping away, buried under all this bloodshed."

Amira reached across the table, placing a hand on his arm. "The bloodshed won't last forever. But the ideas, the vision—that's what will endure. You just need to stay strong, for all of us."

***

Despite the growing toll, the revolution began to see key victories. In the western provinces, a group of miners led a successful rebellion against the imperial forces stationed there, seizing control of a major gold mine. This victory was more than just symbolic—it gave the revolution access to critical resources that would help fund their efforts and keep the movement alive.

In the southern provinces, the rebels managed to gain control of several key towns, creating a network of territories that were effectively outside of imperial control. This allowed the movement to establish safe havens for refugees and rebels, as well as supply lines for food, weapons, and information.

Georgiy's forces also won important battles in the cities. Rebel militias, supported by underground schools and intellectual networks, began to disrupt the empire's control over urban centers. They sabotaged imperial infrastructure, cut off communication lines, and launched targeted strikes against key imperial officials. The revolutionaries had become adept at guerrilla warfare, using the empire's size and slow bureaucracy to their advantage.

These victories, though hard-won, boosted the morale of the revolutionaries and gave them the confidence they needed to push forward. For the first time, it seemed that they might be able to turn the tide against Igor and the imperial forces.

***

With the revolution gaining momentum, Georgiy knew that they needed more than just military victories. They needed allies—both inside and outside the empire. He began to reach out to disaffected nobles, merchants, and foreign leaders, hoping to secure their support for the cause.

Georgiy sent emissaries to the northern provinces, where several noble families had begun to question Igor's leadership. Though these nobles had no love for rebellion, they saw the writing on the wall. The empire was teetering on the brink of collapse, and if they wanted to preserve their power, they would need to side with whoever could ensure the future stability of Ata.

At the same time, Georgiy's diplomats reached out to neighboring nations, hoping to secure trade deals and supplies. They promised that a reformed Ata, led by Georgiy and the ideals of the Space Revolution, would be a better and more prosperous trading partner than the current empire under Igor's rule.

***

As the revolution spread and key victories were won, Georgiy began to feel a fragile sense of hope. The empire was crumbling, and Igor's forces were beginning to show signs of fatigue. But Georgiy knew that the fight was far from over. Igor would not give up easily, and the final confrontation between the two brothers was inevitable.

For now, though, the revolution held strong. The people of Ata had tasted freedom, and they weren't willing to give it up. The fight for the future continued, but with each passing day, Georgiy's vision of a new empire—a better, more just empire—seemed just a little bit closer.

Chapter 28

Brothers at War

Igor's response to the growing rebellion had been swift and brutal. While his early attempts to crush the uprising had been met with resistance, he had learned from those defeats. No longer satisfied with merely punishing pockets of rebellion, Igor now launched a full-scale offensive, determined to wipe out every trace of Georgiy's influence from the empire.

In his war council, Igor addressed his generals, his voice cold and unwavering.

"This is no longer about controlling a few rebellious provinces," he said, staring down the map of the empire spread across the table. "Georgiy has turned this into a war for the soul of the empire. We will respond in kind. There is no room for mercy, no time for negotiations. We will wipe them out, and we will show the people that defiance will be met with absolute force."

His generals, seasoned warriors hardened by years of service, nodded in agreement. Under Igor's leadership, the imperial army had become more than just a military force; it had become a weapon of fear. Cities that had once harbored revolutionaries were burned to the ground, their inhabitants forced to flee or face execution. Villages suspected of supporting Georgiy's cause were destroyed, and any trace of the Za Lyubov movement was hunted down and eradicated.

"Leave nothing behind," Igor ordered as the imperial legions marched out once more, their banners flying high as they descended upon rebel-held territories with terrifying precision.

***

As Igor's army swept across the empire, laying waste to rebel strongholds, the ideological rift between the brothers grew wider. What had once been a conflict of visions—Georgiy's dream of a progressive, educated empire versus Igor's iron-fisted rule—was now a deeply personal war. Each brother had come to see the other not just as an opponent, but as the embodiment of everything they stood against.

To Igor, Georgiy was a fool, blinded by idealism and a naive belief in the power of knowledge. He saw his brother's insistence on peaceful reform as a weakness, a failure to understand the harsh reality of ruling an empire. "You can't build an empire on dreams," Igor thought bitterly as he planned his next campaign. "You build it with strength. With power. And if Georgiy won't see that, then I'll show him what real power looks like."

For Georgiy, the situation was more complex. He still believed in the ideals of education and progress, but he could no longer deny the price they were paying. The revolution was no longer just about ideas—it had become a brutal, bloody war. And while he despised the violence, he knew that retreating now would mean abandoning everything they had fought for. Worse, it would mean leaving the people of Ata at Igor's mercy.

"We didn't start this war," Georgiy said to Amira one evening as they reviewed reports from the front lines. "But we have to finish it. If we give up now, everything we've fought for, everything the people believe in, will be lost."

Amira, ever the pragmatist, nodded. "I know you don't like this, Georgiy. But sometimes, the only way to protect what you believe in is to fight for it."

***

As both sides prepared for what was sure to be the decisive clash, the empire stood on the brink of total collapse. Entire provinces had been lost to the rebellion, and the imperial army, stretched thin by the ongoing campaign, was beginning to show signs of exhaustion. But Igor, driven by his unwavering belief in the necessity of absolute control, refused to relent.

He consolidated his forces for a final push toward the rebel stronghold—a mountainous region in the far south where Georgiy and his followers had regrouped. The stronghold, nestled among the peaks and valleys, was difficult to access, but it was the heart of the revolution. If Igor could take it, the rebellion would fall.

Georgiy, aware of the impending assault, rallied his forces. Despite the brutal toll the war had taken, his followers remained fiercely loyal. The victory at the Space School Academy had given them hope, and now they were ready to fight to defend the future they believed in.

Georgiy stood before them, his voice steady but urgent as he addressed the gathered rebels.

"Igor is coming," he said. "And this will be our greatest test yet. We've faced him before, and we've won. But this time, he's bringing everything he has. We fight for more than just survival. We fight for the future of Ata—the future we want to build, the future our children deserve. We stand together, and no matter what happens, we will not go back to the way things were."

The rebels, many of them armed with makeshift weapons and worn armor, cheered. They knew the odds were against them, but they believed in Georgiy. They believed in the revolution.

***

Unlike in previous battles, where Igor had remained behind the front lines, overseeing strategy and issuing orders from a distance, this time he planned to lead the attack himself. He wanted to be the one to deliver the final blow, to personally crush the rebellion and prove, once and for all, that strength was the only way to rule.

The night before the battle, Igor stood with his most trusted generals, surveying the rebel stronghold from a distance. The mountains loomed high above them, their jagged peaks casting long shadows over the imperial camp.

"They're entrenched," one of his generals remarked. "The terrain will be difficult to navigate. But we have the numbers. We can overwhelm them."

Igor nodded, his eyes fixed on the distant peaks. "I'm not interested in overwhelming them. I want them destroyed. Leave no one alive. Burn the stronghold to the ground. When the people see what happens to rebels, they will never dare rise again."

The general hesitated, but nodded. He had seen Igor's ruthlessness before, but this time, there was something different. A cold, calculated fury burned in Igor's eyes—a desire not just to win, but to annihilate.

"And my brother?" the general asked cautiously.

Igor's lips curled into a thin smile. "Bring him to me. Alive. I want him to see what his revolution has cost."

***

As dawn approached, the air around the rebel stronghold was thick with tension. The imperial forces were massing at the base of the mountains, preparing for their ascent. Georgiy's forces, though outnumbered, had the advantage of terrain, and they were determined to hold their ground.

Inside the stronghold, Georgiy walked the narrow corridors, checking in on his fighters, offering words of encouragement where he could. But inside, he felt a gnawing sense of dread. He knew that this battle could determine the fate of the entire empire—either they would win, and the revolution would continue, or they would fall, and with them, any hope for the future would be extinguished.

Amira found him near the entrance of the stronghold, her face calm but serious.

"They're coming," she said softly. "We're ready, as ready as we can be."

Georgiy nodded, but didn't speak. He looked out toward the mountains, where the imperial banners could be seen in the distance, slowly advancing.

"We've fought so hard for this," he said quietly. "But I wonder... will it be enough?"

Amira placed a hand on his shoulder. "We fight for something bigger than ourselves, Georgiy. And that will always be enough. No matter what happens."

***

As the sun rose over the mountains, the two armies prepared for the final confrontation. On one side, the imperial forces, led by Igor, determined to crush the rebellion and restore order to the empire through fear and violence. On the other, Georgiy's rebels, fighting for a future they believed in, knowing that this might be their last stand.

The battle for the future of Ata was about to begin.

Chapter 29

The Final Battle

The sun had barely risen, casting a pale glow over the jagged peaks surrounding Georgiy's stronghold. The air was cold and still, heavy with the weight of what was to come. In the valleys below, Igor's imperial forces stirred, preparing for their assault. Banners snapped in the wind as thousands of soldiers assembled in formation, their armor gleaming in the early morning light. The sound of boots crunching against the rocky ground and the clang of weapons being readied filled the air, creating an ominous rhythm that echoed through the mountains.

From his vantage point at the edge of the stronghold, Georgiy watched the army move below. His heart pounded in his chest as he scanned the lines of soldiers, knowing that this would be the moment that determined the fate of everything they had fought for. The revolution, the ideals of education, progress, and justice—all of it hung in the balance.

"They're ready for us," Amira said quietly, standing beside him. She looked out over the landscape, her eyes calm but sharp. "We have the high ground, and our people are prepared. But they have the numbers, and Igor is coming for you."

Georgiy nodded, his expression hardening. "I know. We have to hold. If we can withstand the first wave, we might have a chance. But if we break..." He let the thought trail off, knowing that if they failed here, everything would be lost.

"We won't break," Amira said firmly. "Not with you leading us."

***

The first sound of the imperial army's advance was a deep, resonant horn blast that echoed through the valleys like a thunderclap. It was a signal, a call to arms, and as it faded, the imperial forces began their march toward the stronghold.

Georgiy's rebels had taken up defensive positions along the cliffs and ridges surrounding the main entrance to the stronghold. Archers lined the high ground, their bows drawn, waiting for the signal to unleash a hail of arrows on the advancing troops. Below them, lines of soldiers armed with spears, axes, and makeshift weapons stood ready to defend the narrow paths leading up the mountains.

"Archers, hold!" Georgiy commanded, his voice ringing out as the imperial army grew closer. He could see them now, a sea of soldiers moving as one, their shields raised, their swords drawn. The sight was both terrifying and awe-inspiring—an unstoppable wave of power.

The imperial soldiers moved with military precision, forming ranks as they began their ascent up the steep, rocky paths toward the rebel stronghold. Their shields locked together, forming a wall of steel as they climbed, protecting them from the arrows that would inevitably rain down from above.

"Wait for my signal," Georgiy said again, his voice steady as he watched the enemy advance. His own heart raced, but he refused to show any sign of fear. His people were watching him, counting on him to lead them through this.

Finally, when the imperial soldiers were close enough that Georgiy could see the grim determination on their faces, he raised his hand.

"Now!" he shouted.

A volley of arrows shot through the air, a dark cloud that descended upon the advancing imperial forces with deadly accuracy. The first row of soldiers stumbled, some falling to the ground with arrows embedded in their armor, but the rest pushed forward, unde-terred by the losses.

More arrows followed, but still the imperial army pressed on, their shields raised high as they advanced relentlessly toward the rebel lines. The defenders fought fiercely, throwing rocks and hurling spears from the heights above, but the sheer numbers of the imperial army began to tell. Slowly, methodically, they climbed closer to the stronghold.

***

From his position at the rear of the imperial forces, Igor watched the battle unfold. He had always known that this fight would be difficult. The rebels had the high ground, and they were fighting for their lives. But he also knew that numbers—and superior training—would eventually win out. All he had to do was wait for the right moment to strike.

When the imperial soldiers reached the base of the stronghold's defenses, Igor raised his sword, the signal for his elite cavalry to move in. The riders, clad in black armor and carrying the imperial banners, surged forward like a storm, charging up the mountainside with brutal speed and force. The ground shook beneath their hooves as they closed in on the rebels' final line of defense.

Georgiy saw them coming. His heart sank as the cavalry cut through his forces with ruthless precision, their lances piercing through the rebel defenders as though they were made of paper. The lines began to falter, and Georgiy could feel the tide of the battle turning against them.

But even as his forces buckled under the onslaught, Georgiy refused to retreat. He moved down into the fray, fighting alongside his people, wielding his sword with a desperate ferocity. "Hold the line!" he shouted, over and over, his voice hoarse with effort. "We can't let them break through!"

***

Amid the chaos, Georgiy caught sight of Igor. His brother, riding at the head of the cavalry, was leading the charge, his face set in a cold mask of determination. Their eyes met across the battlefield, and in that instant, Georgiy knew that this was it—the moment they had both been heading toward since the revolution began. Everything had led to this confrontation.

With a shout, Georgiy charged toward Igor, cutting through the melee with single-minded focus. Around him, the sounds of battle faded into the background as he zeroed in on his brother. He saw Igor dismount from his horse, sword in hand, and move to meet him.

The two brothers clashed in the heart of the battlefield, their swords ringing out with every strike. It was a brutal, fast-paced duel—one fought not just with steel, but with years of resentment, anger, and unspoken words.

"You've brought this upon yourself, Georgiy!" Igor snarled as their blades met. "You could have walked away! You could have left things as they were. But no—you had to tear everything apart!"

Georgiy gritted his teeth, deflecting Igor's strike. "The empire was already broken, Igor. I'm trying to fix it, to build something better. But you—you'd rather burn everything down than let the people live in peace!"

Igor's eyes blazed with fury. "Peace? You call this peace?" He swung his sword again, harder this time. "You're a fool, Georgiy. You think ideals will save you, but ideals don't win wars. Power does. Strength does!"

"Then you've already lost," Georgiy shot back, blocking another blow. "The people don't want your empire of fear. They want something more—something you'll never understand."

The fight between the brothers raged on, their movements a blur of flashing steel and raw emotion. Both were skilled fighters, but they were also driven by more than just skill—by a need to prove themselves, to settle the conflict that had torn them apart.

As they fought, the battle around them continued to intensify. Rebel and imperial soldiers clashed with equal ferocity, and the mountains echoed with the sounds of war. But despite the chaos, all eyes seemed to be drawn to the two figures at the center of it all—Georgiy and Igor, locked in a deadly dance of fate.

***

The duel seemed endless, neither brother giving an inch. But as the fight wore on, Georgiy began to tire. Igor, fueled by rage and a lifetime of training, pressed the advantage, forcing Georgiy back with each strike. Finally, with a powerful swing, Igor knocked Georgiy's sword from his hand, sending it clattering across the rocky ground.

Georgiy stumbled, breathless, as Igor advanced on him, sword raised for the final blow.

"It's over, Georgiy," Igor said, his voice cold and final. "This is the end of your revolution."

But just as Igor was about to strike, a sharp whistle cut through the air—a signal from one of the rebel commanders. Before Igor could react, a wave of rebel reinforcements surged onto the battlefield, overwhelming the imperial forces and throwing them into disarray.

Igor hesitated, glancing around as his carefully orchestrated battle plan began to fall apart. The rebels, inspired by their new surge of support, pushed back against the imperial lines, driving them further down the mountainside. The tide of the battle was turning once again—this time in Georgiy's favor.

Seizing the moment, Georgiy dove for his fallen sword, rolling to his feet just as Igor turned back toward him. Their eyes met again, and this time, Georgiy saw something new in Igor's gaze—doubt. For the first time, Igor seemed unsure.

"It's not over," Georgiy said, his voice steady despite the chaos around them. "Not yet."

With a roar of determination, Georgiy launched himself at Igor, their swords clashing once more in a final, desperate struggle. This time, it was Georgiy who fought with renewed strength, bolstered by the knowledge that his people were still fighting, still believing in the future he had promised them.

***

As the battle raged on, it became clear that the imperial forces were losing ground. The rebels, driven by their belief in Georgiy's vision and the momentum of their reinforcements, pushed the empire's soldiers back. The once-unbreakable imperial line began to crumble, and one by one, the imperial forces retreated, leaving behind their fallen comrades.

Igor, realizing that the battle was slipping away from him, stepped back, his sword lowered. He stared at Georgiy, his face a mask of fury and disbelief.

"This isn't over," Igor said, his voice low and dangerous. "You may have won today, but the empire will never be yours."

Georgiy, breathing hard but victorious, watched as Igor retreated with his remaining forces. "It's not about the empire, Igor," he said quietly. "It's about the future. And the people will decide what that future looks like."

As the last of the imperial forces withdrew, the battlefield fell silent. The rebels, battered and bruised but still standing, let out a collective cheer of triumph. They had won. For now, the revolution stood victorious.

But Georgiy knew that the fight was far from over. The battle had been won, but the war for the soul of Ata was just beginning.

Chapter 30

Georgiy's Trial

The victory over Igor's forces had been decisive, but Georgiy knew that the revolution's future was still uncertain. The battles had taken a toll on both sides, and now, with the war paused in a tense stalemate, a royal summons arrived. King Sergey himself had ordered Georgiy to return to the capital for an audience—an invitation impossible to refuse.

As Georgiy prepared to leave, Amira stood at his side, her expression a mixture of worry and skepticism. "It's a trap," she warned, pacing the length of their tent. "Igor won't let you walk out of the palace alive. Not after this."

Georgiy remained calm, folding the royal decree. "This is our only chance for peace, Amira. If my father is calling me back, it means he's ready to listen. We've won victories on the battlefield, but if we keep fighting, the empire will collapse, and more people will suffer."

Amira shook her head, her voice sharp. "They don't want peace. They want you dead. If you go, you're giving them exactly what they want."

Georgiy met her gaze, his voice quiet but firm. "If there's even the smallest chance of avoiding more bloodshed, I have to try. I've never wanted war, Amira. This might be our chance to build something better without tearing the empire apart entirely."

After a tense silence, Amira sighed, her shoulders slumping in reluctant acceptance. "Just don't go alone. Promise me that."

"I won't," Georgiy replied. "But this is something I need to face."

***

The journey back to the capital was fraught with tension. Georgiy traveled with a small group of his most trusted companions, including Amira, who refused to leave his side. As they passed through towns and villages ravaged by war, the reality of what the conflict had cost became painfully clear. Fields lay barren, homes abandoned or burned, and the people—those they had sworn to protect—were left in limbo, caught between two warring forces.

When they reached the capital, the city was unnervingly quiet. The streets, once bustling with life, were empty. Citizens watched from the shadows, their faces marked by fear and uncertainty. The very air seemed thick with anticipation as Georgiy and his contingent approached the palace gates.

Upon their arrival, Georgiy was separated from his companions, escorted deeper into the palace by royal guards. The familiar halls of his youth seemed darker now, more foreboding. But rather than being led to the grand throne room where his father would usually hold court, the guards took him down a narrow, winding stairwell that led beneath the palace—into the depths he had never known existed.

The further Georgiy descended, the more oppressive the air became. The stone walls were cold, and the faint flicker of torchlight barely illuminated the passage ahead. It felt as though he were entering a place forgotten by time, a secret that had been buried beneath the empire's grandeur for centuries.

At last, they reached an enormous iron door. Two armored sentinels stood guard, their faces hidden behind thick helmets. One of them knocked, and after a brief pause, the door groaned open.

141

Georgiy stepped through the threshold and into a vast chamber that defied his expectations.

The chamber was a masterpiece of ancient grandeur. Gold-lined walls shimmered in the dim light, and intricate tapestries, depicting the rise of kings and the shaping of empires, adorned every surface. At the center of the room sat a massive throne, but it was the figure upon it that took Georgiy's breath away.

She was immense, radiating a golden glow that seemed to pulse with a life of its own. Her skin gleamed with an ethereal light, and atop her brow sat a third eye, glowing with a penetrating, otherworldly brilliance. Her throne was made of gold and gemstones, but around her, resting in bowls atop pedestals, were glowing golden apples, each one emitting a soft, hypnotic light.

Georgiy stood frozen, unsure whether he was in the presence of a goddess, a queen, or something far older. Before he could gather his thoughts, the figure's three eyes fixed upon him, her voice filling the chamber with a deep, resonant tone.

"Prince Georgiy of Ata," she said, her voice like the rolling of distant thunder. "Do you know who I am?"

Georgiy swallowed, shaking his head. "No," he replied honestly. "I've never seen or heard of you."

The figure smiled faintly, her third eye glowing brighter. "I am Lyubov, the ancient power behind the throne. I have guided Ata for centuries, ensuring its survival and prosperity. Every king you have known has ruled with my counsel, whether they realized it or not."

Georgiy blinked in disbelief. He had heard whispers of ancient powers that controlled the empire's fate, but never had he imagined they were real. And now, standing before him, was the very force that had shaped the empire since its founding.

"You've guided them?" Georgiy asked, his voice hushed with awe.

Lyubov inclined her head. "Yes. Through these apples, I hold the souls of those who have served the empire—the kings, sages, warriors. Their knowledge, their wisdom, their power all reside within me. I ensure that the empire does not falter, that it continues to prosper through the ages."

Georgiy's eyes flicked to the glowing apples. The souls of the dead? The idea made his skin crawl, but he couldn't deny the allure of such power. If this force had sustained the empire for centuries, perhaps it held the key to his own revolution's survival.

Lyubov reached out and lifted one of the golden apples from a nearby pedestal, holding it out toward Georgiy. Its light reflected in her third eye, casting a warm glow across the chamber.

"You seek to change this empire, to lead it into a new age," she said. "I have watched you, and I see promise in your vision. But you must understand—the empire's survival depends on more than ideals. It depends on strength, wisdom, and control. Without me, Ata would crumble."

Georgiy stared at the apple, its golden light mesmerizing. "You control the empire," he said slowly, realization dawning. "Not my father, not Igor—this power is what keeps the empire together."

Lyubov nodded. "Indeed. And now I offer you the same power. Take this apple, and you will gain the wisdom of centuries. The knowledge of kings, warriors, and sages will be yours. With my guidance, you can reshape the empire as you see fit, without the destruction and chaos of war. Together, we can forge a new future for Ata."

Georgiy hesitated. The offer was beyond anything he had imagined. This was the power he had sought—an opportunity to reform the empire from within, without further bloodshed. But accepting it meant embracing the same force that had controlled the empire for so long. Was it worth the price?

As he stood before Lyubov, Georgiy's thoughts raced. He had fought for a future where the people of Ata could determine their own destiny, free from tyranny and oppression. But war had shown him that ideals alone were not enough. The empire was fragile, and without control, without order, it would collapse into chaos. His dream of a better future could only be realized if the empire survived.

He looked up at Lyubov, meeting her gaze. "If I accept, I can bring about the change I've fought for? I can reform the empire, give the people a future built on justice and knowledge?"

Lyubov's smile widened slightly. "Yes. But you must understand that with this power comes responsibility. You will guide the empire, not just as a ruler, but as its protector. Your vision will shape its future, but you must be willing to wield the power necessary to preserve it."

Georgiy took a deep breath, his decision clear. He reached out and took the apple from Lyubov's hand, feeling its warmth radiate through him. As his fingers closed around it, a surge of energy coursed through his body. His mind expanded, and for a moment, he saw beyond the physical world—he saw the souls that inhabited the golden apples, saw the wisdom of ages stretching out before him.

"I accept," he said, his voice steady. "I'll use this power to build the future I've dreamed of, for the people of Ata. But I won't lose myself in it. This is for them, not for me."

Lyubov's eyes gleamed with approval. "Then you have taken the first step toward greatness. You will have my guidance, Georgiy. And together, we will lead Ata into a new age."

As Georgiy consumed the apple, the world around him seemed to shift. His senses heightened, and his mind filled with knowledge—memories of past kings, warriors, and scholars. He saw their triumphs and failures, their struggles to maintain the balance between power and justice. He understood now what Lyubov had meant—power alone wasn't enough. It had to be wielded with care, with wisdom.

When the vision faded, Georgiy stood taller, more resolute. He had the knowledge he needed to lead, to guide the empire through its darkest hour. But now, the burden was truly his to bear.

Georgiy left the chamber, his heart beating with a newfound purpose. As he ascended the winding staircase back to the surface, the weight of the revolution no longer felt as heavy. He had the power to change the empire from within, to bring about the reforms he had dreamed of without resorting to further violence.

Amira was waiting for him at the top of the stairwell, her face lined with worry. "What happened?" she asked, her voice urgent. "What did they want?"

Georgiy paused, glancing back toward the hidden chamber beneath the palace. "I met someone," he said slowly, his mind still processing everything. "Lyubov. She... offered me power, the kind that could change everything."

Amira's eyes widened. "And you accepted?"

Georgiy nodded, his gaze steady. "I did. But it's not what I expected. This power—it's not just for me. It's for the future of Ata. We can still build what we dreamed of, Amira, but now... now I have the means to make it happen."

Amira stared at him, her expression unreadable. "Are you sure about this? That kind of power changes people."

Georgiy met her gaze, a quiet determination in his eyes. "I won't let it. I'll use it to do what we set out to do—to give the people a future they deserve."

Chapter 31

The New Order

With Lyubov's power coursing through him, Georgiy felt a profound shift, both in his perception and in the way the world unfolded before him. The golden apple he had consumed had not only expanded his understanding of leadership and governance, but it had also shown him the threads of the empire's past and its possible futures. For the first time, he saw the fragility of the empire, how tenuous its hold on stability had always been, and why Lyubov's guidance had been so essential to its survival.

But now, the task was his. With this ancient power, he could finally steer Ata into the future he had always envisioned—a future where knowledge, justice, and progress reigned over oppression and fear. He had the tools to bring about the change he sought, but the weight of that responsibility also bore down on him.

When Georgiy returned to his companions, he could see the questions in their eyes, the unspoken doubt and concern about what had transpired in the depths beneath the palace. But he carried with him an air of calm authority, a resolve that had not been there before.

***

The next morning, Georgiy was summoned to the throne room to meet with his father. King Sergey's health had deteriorated further since the last time Georgiy had seen him. His once robust figure had withered, and his skin had taken on a pallor that spoke of his impending mortality. Still, the king's gaze was sharp as Georgiy approached the throne, accompanied by a contingent of nobles who watched with tense anticipation.

Georgiy knelt before his father, feeling the eyes of the court upon him. King Sergey studied his son for a long moment, his expression unreadable.

"You've caused quite the stir, Georgiy," the king finally said, his voice rasping with age. "The people speak of revolution, of change. Some even call you a traitor."

Georgiy rose to his feet, his posture straight, but his tone measured. "I fight for Ata, Father. For the people. The empire you've ruled has been strong, but it's also been cruel. We have the power to be more than just rulers of land and wealth. We can be the leaders of progress, of knowledge. We can build an empire that serves everyone, not just the elite."

King Sergey's gaze darkened slightly. "And you think you're the one to bring this change? You've always had lofty ideals, Georgiy, but ideals don't rule empires. Power does."

Georgiy stepped forward, meeting his father's gaze. "I understand that now. More than I ever did before. But power doesn't have to mean oppression. I've been to the heart of this empire, Father. I've seen its true source."

At that, the king's eyes widened ever so slightly. He understood Georgiy's meaning—he had encountered Lyubov. And if Georgiy had taken her offer, he now wielded a power that few men could comprehend.

King Sergey's expression softened, his voice quiet. "You've spoken with Lyubov, then."

Georgiy nodded. "I have. And I've accepted her guidance. But I'm not here to repeat the mistakes of the past. I'm here to build something new—something better. We can do this together, Father. You've ruled wisely for many years, but it's time to let the empire evolve. Let me guide us into the future."

For a long moment, the room was silent, the tension palpable. The nobles around them shifted uneasily, unsure of what was to come.

Finally, King Sergey sighed, his shoulders sagging with the weight of years and burdens. "You remind me of your mother, Georgiy. She, too, wanted to change the world. Perhaps... perhaps it's time to let you try."

Georgiy's heart swelled with hope, but he kept his emotions in check. "Thank you, Father. Together, we can make this work."

***

Though the king had accepted Georgiy's new role, there was one person conspicuously absent from the court—Igor. Georgiy knew his brother well enough to understand that Igor would not take this quietly. But for now, Igor remained silent, lurking in the shadows, watching as his younger brother ascended to a position of influence within the court.

Days passed without a word from Igor, but Georgiy sensed the growing unrest among the nobility who had once supported his brother. The more conservative members of the court, those who valued tradition over progress, were uneasy with Georgiy's new influence. But none dared openly defy the king's decision to reconcile with his son.

Amira, ever watchful, warned Georgiy that Igor would not stay silent for long.

"He's waiting," she said one evening as they walked through the palace gardens. "Igor's pride won't allow him to let this go. He'll make his move eventually, and when he does, we need to be ready."

Georgiy nodded, his expression thoughtful. "I know. But for now, we need to focus on the reforms. If we can get the people behind us, Igor won't have the support he needs to challenge us."

***

With King Sergey's reluctant blessing, Georgiy began implementing the first of his reforms. He used Lyubov's guidance to navigate the complex political landscape of the empire, carefully balancing tradition with progress. The first major change was the establishment of the Space School Academies, institutions designed to educate children from all social classes in the sciences, medicine, and philosophy.

The academies were a direct challenge to the old order, where education had been reserved for the elite. Now, commoners could learn alongside noble children, gaining knowledge that had once been forbidden to them. These academies became centers of innovation and hope, where students studied astronomy, engineering, and new ideas that would shape Ata's future.

The response from the people was overwhelming. Parents eagerly sent their children to these academies, seeing it as a chance for a better future. Scholars from across the empire flocked to the capital to teach, inspired by Georgiy's vision of an enlightened society.

But not everyone was pleased.

***

As Georgiy's influence grew, so too did the resistance from the noble class. The more traditional nobles, who had prospered under the old ways, saw the new academies as a threat to their power. They feared that the common people, once educated, would demand more rights, more freedom, and that their own privileged positions would be eroded.

Whispers of discontent spread through the court. Some nobles began to speak openly against Georgiy's reforms, accusing him of undermining the stability of the empire. They questioned his loyalty, his motives, and even his sanity for accepting the guidance of Lyubov—an ancient power they had long revered, but never fully understood.

But Georgiy, now armed with the wisdom of Lyubov and the support of the people, was undeterred. He knew that change was never easy, and that those who benefited from the status quo would always resist progress.

Amira was quick to point out the growing danger. "They're plotting against you, Georgiy. You need to be careful. They'll stop at nothing to preserve their power."

Georgiy nodded, his mind already working on the next steps. "I know. But we're not just building schools. We're building a future. And they can't stop that—not if the people stand with us."

***

As the academies flourished, a new generation of thinkers, scientists, and leaders began to emerge. These young minds, unburdened by the rigid traditions of the past, embraced Georgiy's vision of an empire driven by knowledge and progress. They questioned the old ways, challenged the authority of the nobility, and sought out new ideas that could reshape Ata's future.

Georgiy's dream was becoming a reality. Slowly but surely, the empire was changing. But the challenges were far from over. As the reforms gained momentum, so too did the forces working against them. Igor remained silent, but his presence loomed large, and the nobles who opposed Georgiy's vision were growing bolder by the day.

The seeds of the future had been planted, but the storm was not yet over.

Chapter 32

The Eye of Lyubov

Georgiy left the palace quietly, descending once again into the hidden chamber beneath the palace where Lyubov resided. The winding stairwell seemed even darker than before, but Georgiy felt no fear. The power Lyubov had given him had changed him in ways he was still coming to understand.

When he entered the vast chamber, Lyubov was waiting, seated upon her throne of gold and gemstones, her three eyes glowing faintly in the dim light. The golden apples, filled with the souls of Ata's past rulers and warriors, shimmered softly in the bowls around her.

As Georgiy approached, he could sense the weight of the ancient power that still pulsed through the room. He bowed his head respectfully, though he no longer felt the same awe he had during their first encounter. Now, they were partners—bound by the choices he had made.

"You summoned me," Georgiy said, his voice calm but curious.

Lyubov's voice echoed through the chamber, as rich and resonant as ever. "You have done well, Prince Georgiy. The changes you have brought to Ata are significant. But you have only begun to see the challenges that come with true power."

Georgiy looked up at her, his brow furrowed. "I know the nobles are plotting against me. I expected that. But they're not my only concern." He paused. "Igor remains silent, but

I can feel his anger simmering beneath the surface. He's waiting for the right moment to strike."

Lyubov nodded, her three eyes glowing brighter. "You are correct. Your brother's pride has been wounded, and he will not forgive easily. His ambitions for the throne have not faded. But there is more at play than just Igor's resentment. The power you now wield has drawn the attention of others—forces that lie beyond this realm."

Georgiy stiffened. "What do you mean? What forces?"

Lyubov rose from her throne, her towering form casting long shadows across the chamber. Her third eye, glowing with an intense golden light, fixed itself on Georgiy.

"The power that I possess," she began, "is ancient. It has sustained Ata for centuries, and it is connected to forces that stretch far beyond the borders of this empire—forces that govern the balance between worlds. The knowledge I hold is not just the wisdom of past kings and warriors, but the collective consciousness of realms unseen."

Georgiy felt a chill run down his spine. "Realms unseen?" he repeated, trying to grasp the full meaning of her words.

Lyubov inclined her head slightly. "The empire of Ata has been guided by more than mortal rulers. The soul of this empire, the source of its prosperity and power, has always been linked to something greater—something mystical, ancient, and boundless. I am the conduit through which this power flows."

Georgiy's mind raced as he tried to process what he was hearing. He had thought that accepting Lyubov's power meant gaining control over the empire's fate, but now he realized that it was far more complex. The empire was tied to a web of cosmic forces, and he was now part of that web.

Lyubov extended one of the golden apples toward him, and as he looked into its glowing surface, he saw visions—flashes of distant worlds, of ethereal beings whose motives were inscrutable, of conflicts that stretched beyond time itself. He saw the fragile balance that kept Ata's prosperity intact, and he understood how easily that balance could be undone.

"This is the Eye of Lyubov," she said softly. "Through it, you can see beyond the mortal world. You can see the forces that shape our reality, the forces that have guided this empire for ages. But know this, Georgiy—power is not without its cost. You are now bound to the fate of the empire, just as I am. You have the power to shape it, but you must also protect it from the forces that would tear it apart."

Georgiy stared into the apple, feeling the weight of what he had just witnessed. He had sought power to bring change to Ata, but now he saw that the very survival of the empire was dependent on forces he could barely comprehend. He realized that his struggle was no longer just with the nobles, or even with Igor. He was contending with something far larger—a delicate cosmic balance that, if disrupted, could plunge the empire into ruin.

He looked up at Lyubov, his voice tinged with uncertainty. "You gave me this power to guide the empire, but I didn't know... I didn't know I would be responsible for so much more than just the people of Ata."

Lyubov's expression remained serene. "You are a ruler now, Georgiy. Rulers are never only responsible for what they see. Their reach extends far beyond their understanding. The power I have given you comes with the responsibility to protect not only the empire but the balance between worlds."

Georgiy felt the weight of her words settle heavily upon him. "And if I fail?"

Lyubov's third eye flared with light. "If you fail, Ata will fall—not just to your enemies here, but to forces that will tear the empire apart, from the inside out. You are the guardian of this balance now, Georgiy. But you are not alone. I will continue to guide you, but your choices will determine the fate of this empire—and perhaps much more."

Lyubov gestured toward the apple again, and as Georgiy gazed into its surface, he saw a vision of Ata's possible futures. In one vision, he saw a thriving empire, its people united by knowledge and progress, reaching out into the stars as the Space School Academies flourished and the next generation of scholars and explorers led the empire into a new golden age.

But in another vision, he saw a different future—a future where the empire had crumbled, torn apart by internal strife and the unchecked ambitions of those who sought to take power for themselves. In this vision, he saw Igor seated on the throne, ruling over a broken and fearful people, the light of progress extinguished.

Georgiy recoiled from the vision, his heart pounding. "I won't let that happen," he said, his voice shaking with determination. "I'll do whatever it takes to protect Ata from that future."

Lyubov smiled faintly, her eyes gleaming with approval. "Then you are ready. The future is uncertain, but with the power you now wield, you have the ability to shape it. Remember, Georgiy—this power is not just for you. It is for the people of Ata, for their future. Use it wisely."

***

When Georgiy emerged from the chamber, the weight of his new responsibilities pressed heavily upon him, but his resolve was stronger than ever. He had seen the possible futures that awaited the empire, and he knew what was at stake. He would not let Ata fall—not to Igor, not to the nobles, and certainly not to the unseen forces that sought to unbalance the world he had come to protect.

Amira was waiting for him at the entrance to the palace, her eyes filled with questions. "What happened down there?" she asked.

Georgiy hesitated for a moment, still processing the enormity of what he had learned. "I've seen the future, Amira," he said quietly. "And it's both beautiful and terrifying. We have a lot of work to do."

Amira frowned. "You mean the reforms? I know the nobles are pushing back, but—"

"It's not just the reforms," Georgiy interrupted. "It's everything. Ata's future... our future... depends on more than just what happens in the capital. There are forces at play that are far bigger than us, and we have to make sure we don't let them tear everything apart."

Amira studied him carefully, sensing the change in his demeanor. "What are you planning to do?"

Georgiy looked out over the horizon, his eyes filled with determination. "I'm going to protect this empire. But I'll need your help—now more than ever."

Chapter 33

Reconciliation

The next morning, Georgiy summoned his brother to the palace courtyard. It was a risky move, but one that he believed was necessary. The empire could not move forward with the constant threat of internal conflict, and Georgiy knew that if he did not make an effort to resolve the animosity between them, Igor's inevitable uprising could destabilize everything he had worked for.

When Igor arrived, he was flanked by a small group of his most loyal supporters—military officers and nobles who had long sided with him in the hopes of restoring the empire to its former, more oppressive glory. Though the tension in the air was palpable, Georgiy did not allow himself to be intimidated.

Igor stepped forward, his face set in a hard, unreadable expression. His eyes, cold and calculating, met Georgiy's.

"You've summoned me like a prisoner, brother," Igor said, his voice laced with contempt. "I assume you're ready to declare yourself the rightful heir and finish what you started?"

Georgiy shook his head, keeping his tone calm but firm. "No, Igor. I'm not here to humiliate you or claim the throne. I called you here because this division between us is tearing the empire apart. The war is over, but we're still fighting, and it's weakening us from within. We need to find a way to move forward together."

Igor's jaw clenched, and he took a step closer, his fists tightening. "Move forward? With you leading the charge? You, who betrayed the empire, who turned the people against their rightful ruler? You've led a revolution that has undermined everything our family built."

"No," Georgiy replied, his voice firm but not without compassion. "I didn't betray the empire. I fought for its survival—its true survival. The empire can't continue to exist as it once did. The world is changing, Igor, and we need to change with it. I'm offering you a chance to be part of that change."

Igor's eyes flashed with anger, his voice rising. "You speak of change, but all I see is chaos! The people may cheer your name now, but it won't last. They're fickle, Georgiy. They want a strong hand to lead them, not your idealistic nonsense. You think you can rule this empire with schools and science, but when the real threats come, your knowledge won't save them."

Georgiy met Igor's fiery gaze without flinching. "Strength alone won't save the empire either. We've seen what your 'strong hand' has done—it's led to fear, to oppression. You rule with violence and control, and it's tearing the empire apart. We need something more than just strength, Igor. We need to give the people hope, a future they can believe in."

Igor's expression hardened, but Georgiy saw a flicker of doubt in his eyes. For the first time, Georgiy realized that beneath Igor's bluster, there was fear—fear of losing the power and control that had defined his life.

Georgiy stepped closer, his voice lowering but losing none of its intensity. "You don't have to lose your place in this, Igor. We can lead together. I've seen a future where the empire thrives—not through fear, but through knowledge and progress. But I need your help. You're a soldier, a leader. The people still look to you for strength. Let's rebuild this empire together. Not as enemies, but as brothers."

For a moment, Igor stood silent, his fists clenched at his sides, his jaw tight. Georgiy could see the conflict raging within his brother. Igor's entire life had been about control, about power. To give that up, to share it, went against everything he had been taught. But

Georgiy's words had planted a seed of doubt, and for the first time, Igor found himself questioning whether his path—his rigid belief in absolute power—was the right one.

Finally, after what felt like an eternity, Igor spoke, his voice low and measured. "And what would my role be in your vision for this new empire?" His tone was less accusatory now, more curious, as though he were considering the possibility for the first time.

Georgiy met his brother's gaze, sensing the opportunity. "We need leadership, strength, and protection. The people need someone to defend them when threats come from beyond our borders. I'm focused on building the future—on schools, education, and progress—but we still need someone to keep the empire safe, to command its forces. That role is yours, Igor. If you're willing to take it."

Igor's eyes narrowed, but there was no hostility in his expression—only contemplation. "And what of the nobles?" he asked. "They won't support your vision so easily. They'll fight you at every turn."

Georgiy nodded. "Some will. But others will see the value in what we're building. If we stand together, they won't have the strength to oppose us. The people are already behind us. If we show unity, they'll follow."

The silence between them stretched out as Igor considered his brother's offer. It was clear that the old grudges and resentments had not entirely faded, but for the first time, Georgiy sensed that his brother was truly listening.

Finally, Igor let out a slow breath. "I don't trust your idealism, Georgiy. I think you're setting yourself up for disappointment, thinking the world can be ruled by education and progress. But... I'm tired. Tired of fighting, tired of watching the empire bleed."

He paused, his expression hard but thoughtful. "If you're serious about this partnership—if you truly believe that we can rule together—then I'll stand by your side. But make no mistake—I won't let this empire fall because of your dreams. If the time comes for strength, I'll be the first to take command."

Georgiy's heart lifted, but he remained composed. "Then we'll lead together. I promise you that this empire will be stronger, not weaker, for the changes we're making. With your strength and my vision, we can ensure Ata's future."

Igor extended his hand, and after a tense moment, Georgiy took it. The two brothers, once torn apart by their opposing views, stood united—for now. The road ahead would not be easy, and Georgiy knew that Igor's loyalty could shift if he felt threatened. But for the time being, they had reached a fragile truce.

***

With Igor's reluctant support, Georgiy's position within the empire grew even stronger. The nobles, once divided between the two brothers, now found themselves unable to challenge the united front presented by the royal family. The more conservative factions continued to grumble about Georgiy's reforms, but without Igor to rally behind, their influence began to wane.

Georgiy, now more determined than ever, pressed ahead with his reforms. The Space School Academics expanded, new infrastructure projects began, and trade routes were re-established with neighboring regions. Under his leadership, the empire began to recover from the scars of war, slowly but surely transforming into the progressive society he had envisioned.

But in the back of his mind, Georgiy knew that this fragile alliance with Igor was built on shifting ground. The tension between them had not disappeared—it had merely been buried, for now.

Chapter 34

A New Frontier

The academies were not just about teaching traditional subjects like mathematics, history, and literature. Georgiy had always believed that the future of Ata lay in the stars, and so the academies also focused on astronomy and space exploration—disciplines that, until recently, had been considered fanciful dreams. He envisioned an empire that looked beyond its borders, one that would be at the forefront of scientific discovery.

At each academy, students were taught the basics of astronomy and physics. They learned to read the stars, to calculate distances between celestial bodies, and to imagine what lay beyond the familiar sky. Georgiy had personally overseen the recruitment of some of the brightest minds in Ata—scholars who had once been dismissed for their unconventional ideas. Now, these scholars were given the freedom to experiment, to push the boundaries of what was possible.

In the capital, the flagship Space School Academy became a hub for new inventions and ideas. A group of engineers, inspired by Georgiy's vision, had even begun to work on early designs for rockets and exploration vessels—primitive, perhaps, but filled with the potential to one day reach the stars.

Georgiy made regular visits to the academies, offering support and encouragement to the students. He spoke of the future with excitement, telling them that they were not only the future of Ata but the pioneers of an entirely new era of human achievement.

But not everyone shared Georgiy's enthusiasm for the academies. While the common people embraced the opportunity for their children to receive an education, the nobility—particularly those who had been loyal to Igor—viewed the schools with suspicion. The idea of educating commoners, of giving them access to the same knowledge once reserved for the elite, threatened their hold on power.

In the halls of the palace, whispers of dissent continued to circulate. Nobles who had grown comfortable under the old regime worried that the educated masses would soon begin to challenge their authority. For them, knowledge was a dangerous weapon, one that could upend the delicate social hierarchy they had spent generations maintaining.

"This obsession with schools is madness," Lord Kazimir, one of Igor's closest allies, muttered during a private council meeting. "Georgiy is filling the heads of peasants with dangerous ideas. They'll start demanding rights, land, power. We'll have a revolt on our hands."

Igor, who had quietly listened to these complaints in the weeks following his reconciliation with Georgiy, remained outwardly neutral. But in truth, he, too, harbored concerns about the rapid expansion of the academies. Though he had agreed to stand by Georgiy for now, he worried that his brother's idealism was moving too quickly, that Ata was not ready for such radical change.

"The people are already demanding more than they deserve," Kazimir continued, his voice dripping with disdain. "If we continue down this path, we'll have nothing left to rule over."

Igor gave a slow nod, his expression unreadable. "Georgiy's vision is ambitious," he said carefully, choosing his words. "But ambition without limits can be dangerous. I'll speak with him."

***

Later that evening, Igor approached Georgiy in his study. The room was filled with scrolls and maps, many of them detailing plans for the next wave of academies that Georgiy hoped to build across the empire. His enthusiasm was palpable as he outlined his ideas to Amira, who was reviewing the latest reports from the schools.

"You're pushing too hard," Igor said bluntly as he entered the room, his tone betraying his frustration.

Georgiy glanced up, surprised but not entirely unprepared for this confrontation. He had known that the expansion of the academies would create friction with the more conservative factions, but he had hoped that Igor would at least understand the long-term benefits.

"We need to move quickly if we're going to secure the future of the empire," Georgiy replied calmly. "The academies are our best chance to create a society where everyone can contribute to the progress of Ata. If we delay, we'll fall behind."

Igor shook his head, stepping closer. "You're creating unrest among the nobles. They're already questioning your authority—and mine. You think these schools are going to bring about some golden age, but all they're doing is making people restless. They want more than education, Georgiy. They want power. And once they have knowledge, they'll demand it."

Georgiy set down the scroll he had been holding, standing to face his brother directly. "That's exactly the point, Igor. The empire can't survive by holding onto the past. We have to give the people a voice, a chance to shape their own future. Education is the first step."

Igor's eyes narrowed. "And what happens when they turn that voice against you? Against us? You think you're building a new empire, but you might be tearing it down."

Georgiy held his brother's gaze, his voice steady. "The empire will be stronger for it. Yes, there will be challenges, but if we don't change, if we keep ruling through fear and ignorance, the empire will fall. Maybe not today, but soon. I'm trying to prevent that. And I need you to see that, Igor."

There was a tense silence as the two brothers stared at each other, the weight of their shared history and differing visions hanging between them. Finally, Igor exhaled, his expression softening just slightly.

"I see your point, Georgiy. But I still think you're risking too much, too fast. Just... be careful. The nobles are watching, and they won't sit quietly forever."

Georgiy nodded. "I'll keep that in mind. But we can't slow down. There's too much at stake."

***

Despite the resistance from certain factions within the nobility, the academies continued to grow. Within a year, more than a dozen new schools had been established in key provinces, each one modeled after the flagship academy in the capital. Students from across the empire flocked to these institutions, eager to learn and to contribute to the new vision Georgiy had inspired.

The Space School Academies became more than just places of learning—they became symbols of hope. Scholars from neighboring lands came to Ata to teach, bringing with them new ideas and fostering an exchange of knowledge that had not been seen in generations.

For the first time, children of farmers and laborers sat beside the children of nobles, sharing the same lessons, dreaming the same dreams of exploration and discovery. The gap between the classes began to close, slowly but surely, as the people of Ata began to see that education could offer a path to a better future for all.

As the years passed, the first graduates of the academies began to take their place in society. They were bright, ambitious, and unafraid to challenge the status quo. Some became scholars and engineers, pushing the boundaries of what was possible in science and technology. Others became advisors to local leaders, bringing new ideas about governance and justice to their regions.

But it was the young students of astronomy and space exploration who captured the empire's imagination. Inspired by Georgiy's vision of looking beyond the borders of Ata, they began to dream of traveling to the stars, of expanding the empire's reach not through conquest, but through discovery.

***

Though the future of Ata remained uncertain, Georgiy's reforms were beginning to bear fruit. The academies had given the people a taste of what was possible, and now, they wanted more. The empire was changing, and for the first time in generations, the people believed that they could be part of that change.

But as Georgiy stood at the helm of this new order, he knew that the road ahead would not be easy. The forces of tradition, embodied by Igor and the conservative nobles, were still strong, and the challenges they posed were far from over.

Still, as he looked out over the growing empire, Georgiy felt hope. He had planted the seeds of progress, and now it was up to the people of Ata to help them grow.

Chapter 35

The Nobles' Last Stand

As the morning sun cast its golden light over Ata's capital, the city seemed calm—too calm. Beneath the surface, tension simmered, a subtle but undeniable shift in the air. The nobles had been quiet for too long, their whispers of discontent growing louder with each passing day. Georgiy knew that the conservative factions were plotting something, but despite his best efforts to keep the peace, a storm was brewing.

Amira stood beside Georgiy in the palace war room, poring over reports from the provinces. Her sharp eyes scanned the scrolls, looking for any sign of the brewing rebellion.

"Something isn't right," she muttered, pushing a map of Ata's western provinces toward Georgiy. "We've lost contact with several key regions. It's subtle, but their usual shipments of supplies have stopped, and there's been a surge of unusual activity from the noble estates."

Georgiy frowned, leaning over the map. He had been expecting resistance from the nobility, but the attack on one of the academies weeks earlier had been a stark reminder that their opposition was becoming more organized.

"Do we know which nobles are leading this?" Georgiy asked, his tone steady but grave.

Amira nodded, tapping on the map. "Lord Kazimir and his allies. They've been rallying support in the western and northern provinces, quietly building an army. They know they can't challenge us directly in the capital, so they're hoping to destabilize the provinces and draw your attention away from the reforms."

Georgiy's eyes narrowed. "They're hoping to split our forces. If we're tied up dealing with rebellion in the provinces, they think they can gain the upper hand in court."

Amira sighed, folding her arms across her chest. "They've also been sending envoys to Igor. They're trying to sway him, to make him believe that your reforms are weakening the empire. They want him on their side, Georgiy."

Georgiy's heart sank at the mention of his brother. Since their reconciliation, Igor had remained mostly silent, watching Georgiy's reforms with a mixture of suspicion and resignation. He hadn't openly opposed the changes, but he hadn't fully embraced them either.

"Igor..." Georgiy began, his voice trailing off. "I can't let him fall into their hands. If he sides with the nobles, it could tear the empire apart."

***

Later that evening, Igor sat alone in his chambers, deep in thought. The nobles had been relentless, sending emissaries to him every few days, trying to persuade him that Georgiy's reforms were dangerous. They painted a picture of an empire unraveling, weakened by Georgiy's "idealistic" visions of education and equality.

And yet, as Igor had traveled through the provinces, he had seen a different reality. He had visited one of the Space School Academies, and there, among the students, he had seen hope—real hope. The children, once destined for lives of hardship, were now learning astronomy, engineering, and medicine. They were excited about the future, eager to contribute to the empire's new direction.

Igor had stood in the academy's courtyard, watching the students practice with telescopes, their eyes bright with wonder as they mapped the stars. He had never seen anything like it.

But then the nobles' words echoed in his mind: "This is not the empire we built. Georgiy's reforms are too fast, too radical. The people will rise against him when they realize the old ways are gone."

Igor's loyalty was torn. He had always believed in strength, in the power of tradition. But now… now, he was no longer sure. The nobles wanted him to lead a rebellion against his brother, but deep down, he wasn't convinced that Georgiy was wrong. The empire was changing, and maybe—just maybe—that change was for the better.

A knock at the door interrupted his thoughts. One of Lord Kazimir's emissaries entered, bowing low.

"Prince Igor," the man began, his voice smooth and practiced. "The nobles grow restless. They seek your leadership. Ata is on the brink of collapse. You must act now, before it's too late."

Igor clenched his fists. "What exactly do they want from me?"

The emissary smiled, his eyes gleaming. "Lead us. Lead Ata back to its true path. Your brother's vision is flawed. He is too focused on dreams and ideals. The people need a strong hand, someone who can restore the empire's might. With you as ruler, we can bring order to this chaos."

Igor stared at the emissary, his mind racing. He knew the nobles were trying to manipulate him, but their words still stoked his doubts.

"Leave me," Igor said, his voice hardening. "I'll make my decision soon."

The emissary bowed again and left the room, leaving Igor alone with his thoughts once more.

***

The following morning, Georgiy received news of increased noble activity in the western provinces. It was clear now that the nobles were preparing for open rebellion. The reports confirmed what Amira had suspected—Kazimir and his allies were gathering forces, and the provinces were slowly being drawn into their web.

As Georgiy stood in the palace gardens, gazing out over the city, Amira approached him quietly.

"They're pushing for a confrontation," she said softly. "If we don't act soon, they'll force us into a civil war."

Georgiy remained silent for a moment, his thoughts heavy. "I don't want to go down that path, Amira. I've spent my life trying to avoid it. We've come so far, and I won't let this rebellion undo everything we've built."

Amira nodded. "Then what's the plan? We can't just ignore them. If they strike, we'll be caught off guard."

Georgiy turned to face her, his resolve hardening. "We don't ignore them. We reach out. I want to speak with the moderates among the nobles, the ones who haven't fully committed to Kazimir's cause. If we can bring them over to our side, we might be able to defuse this before it turns violent."

Amira looked at him skeptically. "You really think the moderates will listen? Most of them are too afraid of Kazimir to oppose him."

Georgiy sighed. "I know it's a long shot, but I have to try. If we can avoid bloodshed, if we can show the nobles that there's a place for them in this new empire, we can end this rebellion before it starts."

Over the next several days, Georgiy sent emissaries to the more moderate nobles, those who had not fully aligned with Kazimir but still harbored doubts about the reforms. The message was simple: "Ata is changing, and you can either help shape that change or be left behind."

Some of the nobles responded positively, intrigued by the possibility of being part of a new order. Others were more cautious, unsure if they could trust Georgiy's vision. Still, the conversations were a start.

In the midst of these delicate negotiations, a message arrived from one of the provincial academies. It had been attacked—burned to the ground by noble forces loyal to Kazimir. The rebellion had begun.

Chapter 36

A Test of Leadership

The smell of smoke hung heavy in the air as the messenger delivered the news. Another academy, this time in the northern province of Olgad, had been destroyed by rebel forces. The attack was swift and brutal—buildings burned, students scattered, and several teachers killed in the chaos. It was the boldest move yet from the nobles loyal to Lord Kazimir.

Georgiy stood silently in the palace war room, staring at the map of Ata laid out before him. His hands gripped the edge of the table as he listened to the report, his jaw clenched in frustration.

Amira, standing at his side, shook her head. "They've crossed the line. This is no longer just political resistance. They're trying to destroy everything you've built. What are we going to do?"

Georgiy closed his eyes for a moment, taking a deep breath to steady himself. His mind raced with options, none of them appealing. He had tried to reason with the moderates, but the more aggressive nobles had shown they weren't interested in dialogue. They wanted power back, and they were willing to tear the empire apart to get it.

"We can't let this escalate into open war," Georgiy finally said, his voice heavy with resolve. "If we respond with force, it'll only confirm their worst fears—that we've abandoned the old ways entirely."

Amira frowned, pacing the room. "But they've already started the fight, Georgiy. If we don't act soon, they'll burn every academy and rally more supporters in the provinces. You've always wanted to avoid violence, but at what point do we defend ourselves?"

Georgiy turned to her, his eyes hardening. "I know we have to act, but there has to be another way. We've worked so hard to build something better. I'm not going to throw it all away by repeating the same mistakes my father and Igor made. We don't rule through fear. Not anymore."

***

Word of the attacks spread quickly throughout Ata. The conservative nobles who had not yet declared open rebellion were watching closely, waiting to see how Georgiy would respond. Some feared his reforms were weakening the empire's strength, while others remained on the fence, unsure of which side to support.

Meanwhile, in the western provinces, Lord Kazimir was growing bolder. His forces, emboldened by the attacks on the academies, began to seize control of key towns and trade routes, cutting off supplies to the capital. Kazimir believed that if he could isolate Georgiy, he could force a confrontation that would bring down the reformist government.

Kazimir's emissaries continued to press Igor to join their cause. They promised him command of the rebel forces, appealing to his sense of military duty and his belief in a strong, united empire. But Igor remained silent, still unsure of his path.

Late one evening, as the capital simmered with tension, Igor found himself once again in Georgiy's study. He had been watching from the sidelines, observing how his brother handled the escalating crisis. Though he had his doubts, he couldn't deny the impact Georgiy's leadership was having. The people, for the most part, supported the reforms. The academies had become symbols of hope for a future where all could contribute to the empire, not just the elite.

But now, with Kazimir's forces striking out, Igor felt the growing pressure to act. He paced the study, his frustration clear.

"You're too soft, Georgiy," Igor finally said, stopping in front of his brother. "Kazimir is testing you, and if you don't push back, he'll burn everything you've built to the ground. He's already started a war, whether you want to admit it or not."

Georgiy looked up from his desk, meeting Igor's intense gaze. "I know, Igor. But if I react with force, we'll be no better than them. I need to find another way to end this without destroying everything we've fought for."

Igor shook his head, his jaw clenched. "I understand your ideals, but ideals don't win wars. Sometimes, you have to fight for what's right. You think Kazimir is going to sit down and talk this out? He's not. He'll keep attacking, and he'll keep gaining support unless we stop him."

Georgiy stood, crossing the room to face Igor directly. "You think I don't know that? You think I don't want to protect this empire? But I can't do it the way you're suggesting. We've spent years trying to move away from the old ways, from ruling through fear and violence. If I give in now, if I fight Kazimir with force, we lose everything."

There was a tense silence between them, both brothers locked in their opposing views. Finally, Igor exhaled, the tension easing slightly from his frame.

"Then what's your plan?" Igor asked, his voice quieter but still demanding.

Georgiy glanced toward the map of Ata, the weight of his decision heavy on his shoulders.

"I'm going to offer Kazimir a choice," Georgiy said. "He can either sit down at the table and negotiate a peaceful resolution, or he can face the consequences of starting a civil war. I'll reach out to the moderates again, see if they're willing to break from Kazimir's camp. If we can divide them, we might stand a chance at ending this before it gets worse."

The next day, Georgiy sent out emissaries to Lord Kazimir and the other nobles. His message was clear: "Ata is changing, but it doesn't have to come at the cost of your influence. Sit down with us, and we can find a way to preserve your role in the new empire. But if you continue down this path, you will face the full force of the law."

At the same time, Georgiy sent discreet offers to several moderate nobles, urging them to abandon Kazimir's rebellion and join the reformists. He promised them roles in the new government, positions of influence in the academy system, and a say in how the empire would move forward.

The response was mixed. Some moderates, seeing Kazimir's growing power, hesitated to break away. Others, tired of the constant conflict and enticed by Georgiy's offer, quietly reached out to pledge their support. The tide was shifting, slowly but surely.

Several days later, word came back from Kazimir's camp. His response was brief but telling: "Ata does not need to negotiate with traitors. We are the true heirs to the empire's strength, and we will not bow to Georgiy's whims. Prepare for battle."

Georgiy's face darkened as he read the message. Kazimir had made his choice.

Amira, standing beside him, looked grim. "So that's it, then. Kazimir wants war."

Georgiy nodded slowly, his expression resolute. "Then we have no choice but to face him. But we'll do it on our terms. We won't become what they want us to be. If they want to fight, we'll defend ourselves—but we won't fall into their trap."

***

As preparations began to defend the capital and the remaining academies, Georgiy sent a final message to Igor. "I need you with me, brother. Kazimir won't stop until he's torn this empire apart. If we're going to save Ata, we have to stand together."

Igor received the message late at night. He sat in silence for a long time, the weight of his decision pressing down on him. He had seen what Kazimir's rebellion could do, but he had also seen the hope Georgiy's reforms had sparked in the people. The future of the empire rested in his hands, and for the first time, Igor realized that the strength Ata needed wasn't just military—it was unity.

Chapter 37
Igor's Choice

The tension in the air was palpable as Igor sat alone in his chambers, staring at the letter from Georgiy that lay on the table before him. Outside, the capital buzzed with preparations for a possible siege. The people were nervous, the soldiers were on edge, and rumors of Lord Kazimir's growing strength spread through the city like wildfire.

Igor's mind was a storm of conflicting emotions. He had spent his life believing in the necessity of strength, of discipline, and of ruling with a firm hand. Kazimir and his allies echoed those beliefs, telling Igor that only a strong, centralized power could keep the empire from crumbling. But Georgiy—his own brother—offered a different path. A path of reform, progress, and cooperation.

The two visions for the future of Ata could not have been more different. And now Igor had to make a choice. Would he stand by Kazimir and the nobles, defending the empire's old ways? Or would he join Georgiy, embracing a future he still wasn't sure he believed in?

Igor rose from his seat and walked to the window, looking out over the city. In the distance, he could see one of the Space School Academies, its domed roof reflecting the fading light of the afternoon sun. He had visited that academy just a few days earlier, speaking with students and teachers who were deeply committed to building Ata's future. For the first time, Igor had felt a flicker of something new—hope, perhaps—that the empire didn't have to be locked in its old traditions.

But he also felt the weight of the nobles' expectations pressing down on him. Lord Kazimir had been clear in his demands. If Igor joined their cause, they could restore Ata's strength and power. If not, they would consider him an enemy, just like Georgiy.

There was no more time to hesitate. The empire needed a leader, and Igor needed to decide where his loyalties truly lay.

***

Later that evening, as the palace prepared for another tense night, Georgiy stood on the balcony overlooking the city. The streets below were quiet, but the stillness did not bring peace. The rebellion was moving closer with each passing day, and despite his efforts to negotiate, Kazimir had made it clear that he was ready for war.

Amira approached from behind, her footsteps soft against the stone floor. "Any word from Igor?" she asked, her voice low.

Georgiy shook his head, his expression grim. "Nothing. I sent him the message, but he hasn't responded. I don't know what to expect anymore."

Amira sighed, folding her arms. "We can't wait forever. Kazimir's forces are closing in, and we need to know where Igor stands. If he sides with the nobles, we'll be facing a two-front war."

Georgiy turned to face her, his eyes filled with uncertainty. "He's my brother, Amira. I know he's struggling, but I can't believe he would turn against me. Not after everything we've been through."

Amira's gaze softened. "I know. But we need to be prepared. This rebellion won't wait for Igor to make up his mind."

***

That night, Igor stood at the edge of the palace courtyard, watching as the soldiers prepared for the coming conflict. The clanging of armor and the steady march of boots echoed through the darkness, a reminder of the battle that loomed just beyond the horizon.

Suddenly, a figure approached—one of Kazimir's emissaries, dressed in dark robes and carrying an air of quiet confidence. The man bowed slightly, his voice smooth and persuasive.

"Prince Igor," he began, his tone respectful. "Lord Kazimir sends his regards. He wishes to remind you that the time to act is now. The empire needs strong leadership, and you are the only one who can provide it. Your brother's vision is misguided—he's weakening Ata, not strengthening it."

Igor remained silent, his face unreadable.

The emissary pressed on. "The nobles are prepared to rally behind you. They trust in your strength, your discipline. With you at the helm, we can restore order to the empire, bring back the glory it once had. But you must make your decision quickly. The window of opportunity is closing."

Igor looked at the man, his expression hardening. "And what will happen if I refuse?"

The emissary's eyes darkened. "Then you will be treated as an enemy of the empire, just like your brother. You will be standing in the way of progress—and you know what that means."

Igor clenched his fists. He had expected as much. The nobles were not offering him a choice—they were giving him an ultimatum. Either he joined them, or he would be cast aside, branded as a traitor to the very cause he had once believed in.

But in that moment, something inside Igor shifted. The words of the emissary—so focused on strength and power—suddenly felt hollow. For so long, Igor had believed that strength was the only way to rule, but now, as he thought about the academy students and the progress they represented, he realized that there was another kind of strength. The strength to build, to create, to inspire.

His brother's vision—one that embraced both knowledge and unity—was not a sign of weakness. It was a path forward, a path that Ata desperately needed.

Igor looked the emissary in the eye, his voice cold and unwavering. "Tell Kazimir I will not join him. I stand with Georgiy."

The emissary's eyes widened in shock, but before he could respond, Igor turned and walked away, his decision made. He was going to fight for the future, alongside his brother.

As dawn broke the next morning, Georgiy received an unexpected visitor. Igor entered the war room, his face set in determination.

Georgiy stood, surprised. "Igor... I didn't expect—"

"I'm with you, Georgiy," Igor interrupted, his voice steady. "Kazimir offered me a way out, a chance to lead the rebellion. But I won't take it. I've seen what you're building. I've seen the future you're fighting for, and it's worth fighting for. You have my support, brother."

Georgiy's heart lifted, relief washing over him. "Thank you, Igor. I knew you'd make the right choice."

Igor nodded, though his expression remained serious. "Don't thank me yet. Kazimir won't take this lightly. He'll come for us with everything he has. We need to be ready."

Georgiy glanced at Amira, who gave him a small nod of approval. "We'll be ready," he said, turning back to Igor. "Together, we'll face whatever comes."

With Igor now fully committed to Georgiy's cause, the brothers immediately began strategizing. Igor's knowledge of the military and the nobles' tactics would be invaluable in the fight against Kazimir. For the first time in weeks, Georgiy felt that they had a real chance of winning—not just the battle, but the future they both wanted for Ata.

The plan was simple but bold. They would rally the loyal forces to defend the capital and the remaining academies, using the city's defenses to their advantage. Meanwhile, Georgiy sent emissaries to the provinces, calling for unity among the people and urging them to reject Kazimir's rebellion.

The message was clear: this was not a fight between brothers. It was a fight for the soul of Ata.

As the city braced for the coming conflict, Georgiy and Igor stood side by side on the palace balcony, overlooking the city they had both sworn to protect.

"Do you think we can win this?" Igor asked quietly, his gaze fixed on the horizon.

Georgiy took a deep breath, his voice calm but resolute. "We don't have a choice. We have to win. For Ata's future."

Igor nodded, his doubts fading as he looked at his brother. For the first time in years, he felt at peace with his decision. They would face Kazimir together, and whatever the outcome, they would face it as a united front.

Chapter 38
The Battle for Ata

The day had arrived. The people of Ata woke to the sound of marching feet and the low, distant hum of war drums. Kazimir's forces, gathered over months of quiet rebellion, were advancing on the capital. Word had spread quickly across the empire—this would be the battle that decided the fate of Ata.

Inside the capital, the tension was palpable. Soldiers lined the city walls, preparing for the worst. Civilians took shelter in their homes, many uncertain about what the future would bring. But amidst the fear, there was also hope. Georgiy's reforms had touched the lives of so many, and the people had seen glimpses of the brighter future he promised. Now, they stood behind him, united in their desire to see the empire move forward, not backward.

In the palace war room, Georgiy, Igor, and Amira finalized their strategy. They had limited forces, but they were loyal. They had the advantage of knowing the city and its defenses, and with Igor now firmly by Georgiy's side, the brothers were determined to face whatever came their way.

"Kazimir is arrogant," Igor said, pacing as he spoke. "He's convinced that we'll crumble the moment his forces breach the city walls. He thinks we'll panic, but we won't. We know this city. We know its strengths and weaknesses."

Georgiy nodded, studying the map of the city before them. "We'll need to draw his forces into the city. If we can keep them away from the academies and the key infrastructure, we stand a chance of holding them off."

Amira, leaning over the map, pointed to the outer gates. "We can use the old city walls to funnel them into the narrower streets. If we position our archers and forces strategically, we can force them into choke points. It'll give us a better chance to limit their numbers."

Igor agreed. "Kazimir's men are strong, but they're undisciplined. They rely on brute force, and that's exactly what we'll exploit. We need to stay calm, stay focused, and use their impatience against them."

***

By midday, Kazimir's forces had reached the outskirts of the capital. From his position on a nearby hill, Kazimir surveyed the city. His army stretched out behind him, an impressive and fearsome sight. The soldiers, hardened by months of rebellion, were eager for the fight. They believed in Kazimir's promise of a return to the empire's former glory, and they were prepared to crush anything that stood in their way.

Kazimir himself stood tall, his eyes narrowing as he watched the capital's defenses. "They've grown weak," he muttered to his second-in-command. "Georgiy's reforms have made them soft. They'll crumble when we strike. And once we take the city, the empire will be ours."

He raised his hand, signaling the advance. The drums of war grew louder as his forces marched toward the city gates.

***

Inside the city, the sounds of Kazimir's army reached the defenders on the walls. The soldiers of the capital—many of them young and untested—looked to their leaders for guidance. But as they saw Igor, fully armored and standing tall beside his brother, their resolve strengthened.

"Hold the line!" Igor called out, his voice carrying across the walls. "Kazimir wants to break us, but we won't let him. This city is our home. We defend it for our families, for our future, for Ata!"

The soldiers cheered, their confidence bolstered by Igor's presence.

As Kazimir's forces reached the gates, the first volleys of arrows flew from the city walls. The battle had begun.

Kazimir's forces pressed hard against the outer defenses, but as Igor had predicted, their brute force approach left them vulnerable. Georgiy's soldiers, positioned strategically along the narrow streets, funneled the enemy into carefully laid traps. Archers rained arrows down from the rooftops, and small, disciplined units of infantry struck swiftly from behind barricades before retreating to the next defensive position.

Despite the chaos of battle, Georgiy remained focused. He moved between the city's defenses, checking on the wounded and encouraging the soldiers. This wasn't just a fight for survival—it was a fight for the future of Ata. The ideals that Georgiy had fought so hard for were being tested, and he would not let them fall.

Amira, meanwhile, led a small contingent of fighters through the city, ensuring that Kazimir's forces didn't breach the academies. The academies had become the heart of the new Ata, and if they fell, so too would the symbol of everything Georgiy had worked to build.

As the battle raged on, Kazimir grew frustrated. His forces were being held back by the city's defenses, and his plan to overwhelm the capital was faltering. Desperate to turn the tide, he ordered his elite soldiers to break through and storm the palace.

"Georgiy won't be able to defend himself once I take the palace," Kazimir snarled. "We'll strike at the heart, and the rest of the city will fall."

Kazimir's elite forces advanced, cutting their way through the outer defenses and making their way toward the palace. But as they approached, they were met by Igor and his personal guard. The two forces clashed in a brutal melee just outside the palace gates.

Igor fought with the ferocity of a man determined to protect his home and his family. His sword flashed in the afternoon sun as he cut down enemy after enemy, holding the line against Kazimir's elite.

As the battle reached its peak, Georgiy knew that the time had come to face Kazimir directly. Leaving the defense of the city to Amira and Igor, he rode out to meet Kazimir on the battlefield.

Kazimir, bloodied but still standing, watched as Georgiy approached. His eyes narrowed, filled with hatred. "You've made a fool's choice, Georgiy," Kazimir spat. "This empire was never meant for your kind of leadership. You've made it weak with your reforms, your so-called progress. Ata was built on strength, and you've stripped it of its power."

Georgiy dismounted and stood before Kazimir, calm despite the chaos around them. "You're wrong, Kazimir," he said quietly but firmly. "Strength doesn't come from ruling through fear. It comes from the people. Look around you. This empire is strong because it's united—not by force, but by hope. Your way is the past. It's over."

Kazimir sneered. "You think you've won, but the people will never follow you. They need someone who can lead them with a firm hand, not a dreamer."

Georgiy's eyes hardened. "I'm not just dreaming, Kazimir. I'm building something real. Something that will last. And it doesn't include you."

Without warning, Kazimir lunged at Georgiy, his sword aimed at his heart. But Georgiy was ready. He sidestepped the attack and parried with a swift, controlled movement, knocking Kazimir's sword from his hand.

Before Kazimir could recover, Georgiy raised his blade, holding it at Kazimir's throat. "It's over, Kazimir. Surrender."

For a moment, Kazimir's eyes flickered with rage, but then his shoulders sagged in defeat. He knew he had lost—not just the battle, but the future of Ata.

With Kazimir captured, the rebellion quickly fell apart. His forces, demoralized and leaderless, surrendered to Georgiy's soldiers. The city was safe, and the ideals that Georgiy had fought for had been preserved.

In the days that followed, Georgiy, Igor, and Amira worked tirelessly to restore order to the empire. The rebels who had followed Kazimir were given a choice: accept the new reforms and be pardoned, or face exile. Most chose to join the new order, realizing that Georgiy's vision for Ata was the only path forward.

***

As the sun set on the day of the final battle, Georgiy and Igor stood together on the palace balcony, looking out over the recovering city. The rebellion had been quashed, but the real work of rebuilding was only just beginning.

"I have to admit," Igor said, his voice thoughtful, "I wasn't sure this would work. I thought Kazimir's way was the only way to keep the empire strong."

Georgiy glanced at his brother, a small smile playing on his lips. "And now?"

Igor sighed, leaning on the balcony rail. "Now I see that strength isn't just about control. It's about giving people the chance to build something better. What you've started here… it's different, but it works."

Georgiy nodded, his heart swelling with hope. "I couldn't have done it without you, Igor. This was never just about me. It's about all of us."

Igor turned to face Georgiy fully, his expression serious. "I'm with you, Georgiy. Let's build this future together."

For the first time, Georgiy felt a deep sense of peace. The old ways were behind them, and the future of Ata was something they would build—not with force, but with unity.

Together, the brothers looked toward the horizon, ready to lead Ata into a new era.

Chapter 39
A New Era Begins

Over the next several weeks, the capital buzzed with activity as the people and soldiers worked together to rebuild what had been damaged during the rebellion. Georgiy led efforts to restore the academies that had been attacked, ensuring that they would once again be places of learning and innovation. He visited each one personally, speaking to the teachers and students, reminding them that they were the heart of the new Ata.

"You are the future," he told a group of students at the Space School Academy. "What we've fought for—what we've built—it's for you. For the generations to come. You'll be the ones to carry Ata forward, to take us to new heights."

The students, many of them still shaken by the conflict, looked up at Georgiy with a sense of pride and determination. The academies had survived, and with them, the dream of a brighter future for Ata.

Igor, meanwhile, focused on ensuring the empire's defenses were secure, but his approach had changed. No longer driven by a need to control through fear, Igor now saw his role as one of protection—not just of territory, but of the people and their newfound freedom. He worked closely with the military, restructuring it to reflect the new ideals of the empire. Soldiers were trained not just as warriors but as guardians of the peace, with an emphasis on service and community.

"We're not just defending the empire from external threats," Igor told his commanders. "We're defending the future Georgiy has built. It's our duty to ensure that no one—inside or outside of Ata—can take that away."

***

One of Georgiy's most significant reforms was the restructuring of Ata's governance. With the rebellion over and the nobles' power diminished, Georgiy seized the opportunity to create a system that would balance power between the people, the military, and the scholars.

The Council of Unity was formed—a body made up of representatives from each province, elected by the people, alongside appointed scholars from the academies and experienced military leaders. This council would work together to shape policy, ensuring that the needs of all citizens were considered, not just those of the elite.

Georgiy sat at the head of the council, but his leadership was no longer absolute. Instead, he served as a guide, ensuring that the principles of progress, education, and equality were upheld in every decision. The council's first meetings were focused on repairing the damage caused by the rebellion and laying the groundwork for the future.

"This council is a symbol of the new Ata," Georgiy said during the inaugural session. "No longer will power be concentrated in the hands of a few. From now on, the people of Ata will have a voice in their future. This is how we build lasting peace."

The creation of the council was met with mixed reactions from the remaining nobles, many of whom still held onto their titles and lands. But Georgiy, with Igor's support, made it clear that the old ways were no longer sustainable. The council's decisions would guide Ata into the new age, and those who resisted would be left behind.

***

One of the most exciting developments in the new Ata came from the scholars and engineers at the Space School Academies. Georgiy's vision for Ata had always included looking beyond the borders of the empire—beyond even the stars. But unlike the tales of space exploration he once dreamed of, the first step toward understanding the cosmos would not come from ships that sailed the skies, but from telescope technology that allowed people to see farther than they ever had before.

In one of the capital's academies, a group of scholars had been working tirelessly on this new invention. The telescope, though crude in its early form, represented the first significant leap in Ata's ability to understand the heavens. It was a device capable of magnifying distant celestial bodies, bringing the stars, the moon, and even planets into sharper focus.

The excitement surrounding the invention was palpable. For centuries, the people of Ata had gazed up at the stars, wondering what lay beyond. Now, for the first time, they would be able to study the universe with unprecedented clarity.

On the day the telescope was ready to be demonstrated, a crowd gathered at the Space School Academy. Scholars, students, and citizens alike stood in awe as the new invention was unveiled.

Georgiy and Igor were there as well, standing side by side as the lead scholar explained the mechanics of the telescope.

"This is just the beginning," the scholar said, his voice trembling with excitement. "With this device, we will be able to map the stars, study the movements of the planets, and perhaps one day, understand the forces that shape the cosmos itself."

The crowd murmured in anticipation as the scholar pointed the telescope toward the sky, adjusting its lenses to focus on a distant star cluster.

When it was Georgiy's turn to look through the telescope, he held his breath as the stars came into view, clearer and more vivid than he had ever seen them before. It was a humbling experience, one that reminded him of the vastness of the universe and Ata's place within it.

"This is incredible," Georgiy whispered, stepping back from the telescope. "We're seeing farther than we ever thought possible."

Igor, standing beside him, nodded in agreement. "It's a powerful reminder of how much more there is to discover. We've been so focused on what's happening here, in the empire, but this... this opens up a whole new world of possibilities."

Georgiy smiled. "And it's just the beginning. This is what we've been working toward—not just progress within Ata, but a deeper understanding of the world around us."

The invention of the telescope marked a turning point in Ata's pursuit of knowledge and exploration. It wasn't just a technological achievement—it was a symbol of the empire's new direction. Scholars began using the device to chart the stars and study planetary movements, and soon, a new field of study emerged: astronomy.

The telescope became the centerpiece of the Space School Academies' curriculum. Students, inspired by the possibility of understanding the universe, flocked to the academies to learn how to use the device and contribute to the growing body of astronomical knowledge.

Within a few months, the first star charts produced by Ata's scholars were distributed across the empire, bringing the mysteries of the cosmos to the people in a way that had never been possible before. The stars, once distant and unknowable, were now being mapped and understood.

***

That evening, after the telescope demonstration, Igor found himself alone, standing on the balcony of the palace and gazing out over the city. The past few months had changed him more than he had ever thought possible. For so long, he had believed that strength came from power, from control. But now, he saw that true strength came from unity, from the willingness to build rather than destroy.

The empire he had once thought needed to be ruled with an iron fist was flourishing under Georgiy's leadership. The people were hopeful, the academies were thriving, and Ata was no longer bound by the oppressive traditions of the past.

Igor couldn't help but think back to the moment he had been offered the chance to lead the rebellion. He had been so close to making a choice that would have plunged the empire into darkness. But now, standing here, seeing what his brother had built, Igor knew he had made the right decision.

Georgiy joined him on the balcony, the night air cool against their skin. For a moment, neither spoke, content to enjoy the peace they had fought so hard to achieve.

"I wasn't sure we'd get here," Igor finally said, his voice soft. "But we did. You did."

Georgiy smiled, glancing at his brother. "We did. Together."

Igor nodded, a sense of calm settling over him. "I'm proud of what we've built. And I'm ready to keep building."

The two brothers stood in silence, watching as the stars twinkled above them, symbols of the vast, unknown future that lay ahead. The empire was changing, evolving, and for the first time, it was doing so with the strength of its people and the vision of its leaders—together.

As the weeks turned into months, Ata continued to grow and prosper. The Council of Unity worked diligently to ensure that the people's voices were heard, and the Space School Academies flourished, producing a new generation of scholars, scientists, and explorers. The empire had been transformed, but the journey was far from over.

Georgiy and Igor knew that challenges still lay ahead. There would always be those who resisted change, who clung to the old ways. But with the support of the people and the strength of their shared vision, they were confident that Ata's future was brighter than ever.

Chapter 40

A United Future

The streets of the capital, once filled with whispers of fear and rebellion, now buzzed with activity and hope. Markets were bustling, academies were full, and for the first time in generations, the people felt as though they had a say in their own future.

Georgiy had insisted on opening new channels of communication between the government and the people, encouraging open forums and public assemblies. These gatherings, where citizens could voice their concerns, share their ideas, and engage with members of the Council, became central to the new governance of Ata.

One afternoon, Georgiy attended one of these assemblies in the heart of the capital. It was held in an open square, where citizens of all backgrounds—farmers, merchants, scholars, and laborers—gathered to discuss their visions for the future.

As Georgiy listened to a young woman speak passionately about her desire to become an engineer and contribute to the space exploration efforts, he smiled. This was what he had dreamed of—a people inspired not by fear, but by possibility

While Georgiy focused on the Council and the future of education and exploration, Igor had fully embraced his role as the protector of this new Ata. His military background and strategic mind had become invaluable, not for waging war, but for maintaining peace. He was the one who ensured that the military was restructured to defend the people, not oppress them, and his efforts to modernize Ata's defenses were widely respected.

Igor had also become a mentor to the next generation of military leaders. His training camps were renowned for their emphasis on honor, discipline, and responsibility. He no longer taught that strength came solely from the sword, but from the mind and heart as well.

In his downtime, Igor often visited the academies, speaking to students about the balance between progress and protection. He would tell them of the mistakes made in the past—how blind loyalty to tradition and power had nearly destroyed the empire—and how they, the youth of Ata, could ensure that never happened again.

One day, as Igor watched a group of students working on an early model of a space exploration vessel, one of the younger boys approached him timidly.

"Prince Igor, do you really think we'll reach the stars one day?" the boy asked, his wide eyes filled with wonder.

Igor knelt beside him, placing a hand on his shoulder. "Yes," he said quietly but confidently. "I believe we will. And you'll be one of the ones to lead us there."

***

Despite all the progress, there was still one lingering question that weighed on Georgiy's mind—the legacy of Lyubov. The ancient power that had guided the empire for centuries was no longer the central force behind Ata's prosperity, but her presence still loomed in the background. Though Georgiy had chosen to lead the empire into a new era without relying on her mystical influence, the connection between Ata and the cosmic forces that had shaped it for so long could not be entirely severed.

One evening, as the city slept, Georgiy found himself drawn once again to the depths beneath the palace, where Lyubov still resided. The chamber was much as he had remembered it—grand and filled with a golden glow—but the power that had once dominated the space now felt distant, as if the old ways were retreating to make room for the new.

Lyubov, still seated on her throne, regarded Georgiy with her three glowing eyes, though her aura was no longer as imposing as it had once been.

"You have done well, Georgiy," she said, her voice echoing softly through the chamber. "The empire thrives under your leadership. You have taken it down a path I did not foresee."

Georgiy stepped forward, his gaze unwavering. "Ata's future is in the hands of its people now, Lyubov. The days of relying on the past are over."

Lyubov nodded slowly, her expression unreadable. "So it seems. But know this, Georgiy—though you have moved beyond the old ways, the forces that have shaped this empire are still present. The balance you now maintain is delicate. You must remain vigilant."

Georgiy didn't flinch. "I know. The future isn't guaranteed, but we've built something strong—something that will endure."

Lyubov gave him a faint smile. "Then I will watch from the shadows, as I always have. But the choices you make will determine whether Ata rises to the stars... or falls to the dust."

With that, Georgiy turned and left the chamber, knowing that while Lyubov's influence had diminished, the empire's future was now truly its own.

***

To mark the end of the rebellion and the beginning of a new era, a grand celebration was planned in the capital. It was to be the largest gathering Ata had seen in generations—a festival that would celebrate not only the unity of the empire but also the success of the reforms that had transformed it.

The city square was decorated with banners and flowers, and people from all across the empire traveled to the capital to take part in the festivities. The academies showcased their latest innovations, the Council held public forums to discuss the next steps in Ata's future, and the streets were filled with music, dancing, and laughter.

On the final day of the celebration, Georgiy and Igor stood before the gathered crowd, addressing the people who had stood by them through the trials of the past few years.

"Today, we celebrate not just victory, but unity," Georgiy said, his voice carrying over the square. "We have shown that strength comes from working together, from believing in a shared vision for the future. This is only the beginning of what we can achieve, and I am proud to stand with you all as we continue to build the Ata we dream of."

Igor stepped forward, his presence commanding but no longer imposing. "My brother speaks the truth," he said. "We have learned from the mistakes of the past. Ata's strength lies not in the sword, but in its people. And as long as we are united, there is nothing we cannot accomplish."

The crowd erupted into cheers, their voices echoing through the city. The celebration continued long into the night, with the people of Ata reveling in the hope and possibility of the future.

As the festival drew to a close, Georgiy and Igor found themselves once again on the palace balcony, watching the stars twinkle in the night sky. The future they had envisioned—one of education, progress, and unity—was finally within reach. The old empire had been laid to rest, and in its place, a new Ata had been born.

"Do you think we're ready for what comes next?" Igor asked, his gaze fixed on the stars above.

Georgiy smiled, his heart light with hope. "We are. We've built something strong, and we'll continue to build. The people believe in it. And now, together, we'll reach even further—beyond what we ever thought possible."

Igor nodded, feeling a sense of peace he hadn't known in years. "To the stars, then."

"To the stars," Georgiy echoed, as they stood side by side, looking forward to the future they would build together.

AFTERWORD

Dear Readers,

Thank you for joining me on this journey through *Fruits of the Gods*. This story is a blend of tradition and progress, of power and compassion, and at its heart, it reflects the hopes and dreams we all share for a better future. Through the tale of Georgiy and Igor, we've seen how unity, vision, and courage can reshape not just an empire, but the lives of all who live within it.

At the core of this book is a belief in education, opportunity, and the boundless potential of the human spirit. Our mission, *"Za Detey – For Kids! Za Lyubov – For Love! Live, Make, & Enjoy!"*, guides our efforts to build a future where everyone has access to learning and growth. As part of this vision, we are working towards initiatives that support under-privileged children in gaining access to education, with the dream of one day establishing space academies that open the door to the stars for all.

Every time you purchase this book, you're not just experiencing the story—you're helping to make these dreams a reality. Your support is driving us closer to a world where children everywhere can explore their full potential, and where progress and innovation benefit all.

Thank you for being a part of this journey. Together, we are building a future full of hope, discovery, and opportunity for generations to come.

Proudly sponsored by GarbuzSpace.com

Za Detey – For Kids!

Za Lyubov – For Love!

Live, Make, & Enjoy!